FULFILMENT

A sensitive, intensely dramatic story of a woman's search for fulfilment in love...

When her first marriage had gone on the rocks, she had sworn to herself it would never happen again. She and David had been so young, so unfitted to the monumental task of marriage and parenthood. The baby had died and so had the marriage. Now after six years of her second marriage she was again standing at the crossroads...

FULFILMENT

Fulfilment

by

Patricia Robins

Dales Large Print Books
Long Preston, North Yorkshire,
BD23 4ND, England.

British Library Cataloguing in Publication Data.

Robins, Patricia
  Fulfilment.

    A catalogue record of this book is
    available from the British Library

    ISBN   978-1-84262-661-0 pbk

First published in Great Britain in 1993 by
Severn House Publishers Ltd.

Cover illustration © Ricardo Demurez by arrangement with
Arcangel Images

Published in Large Print 2009 by arrangement with
Claire Lorrimer

Dales Large Print is an imprint of Library Magna Books Ltd.

Printed and bound in Great Britain by
T.J. (International) Ltd., Cornwall, PL28 8RW

CHAPTER ONE

1962

'If you feel so dissatisfied with our marriage, I don't know why you stay with me. These constant rows are getting me down, Miranda, so don't imagine you're the only one who is fed up. I think it would be a hell of a lot better for us both if we separate for a while.'

The man's mouth was taught with anger. In repose, the lips were sensitive but not sensuous. Usually, the brown eyes were kind, humorous, gentle, but now irritation made them seem hard and overbright.

He avoided looking at his wife's face. He was always hurting her, failing her in some way and he was unwilling to read the reproach he knew would be in those incredible aquamarine-blue eyes.

Damn her! he thought. She's always making me say things I don't mean. I suppose I'll have to apologize...

But his indignation was deep-rooted, born of a sense of injustice and he couldn't retract. No – not yet.

The moment of silence while she waited

for him to do so passed. Her charming mouth twisted into a painful grimace.

'Very well, John, if that's what you want...'

'I didn't say *I* wanted it. I said I thought it would be best since I've so obviously failed to make you happy.'

Her finely-etched brows lifted for an instant as she turned a thoughtful gaze upon him.

'I can't deny that,' she decided; and then suddenly, was appalled by the seriousness of their words.

People who have loved and laughed together for six years don't break up their marriage in as many minutes, she told herself.

What had started this particular row? An insignificant row blown up from nowhere. John had blamed her for the loss of a favourite tie as they were dressing to go out to a dinner-dance. She was not guilty and had replied coldly that he was no child but quite old enough to look after his own things.

'I'm your wife not your valet!'

After that he'd retired into one of those angry silences that she found so exasperating.

Later, in the bar, they had forgotten the quarrel over cocktails. John had admired the new dress she was wearing and she'd listened to a very dull account of his firm's Board Meeting without once interrupting.

But the earlier disharmony was buried

only just below the surface. After dinner, Miranda wanted to dance. John didn't feel like it. Annoyed by his refusal she had flung a reproach at him.

'What's the point in bringing me to a place where there's a first-class band if you won't dance. You know I come for the dancing more than the dinner.'

Maybe if he had said just a few words, such as 'Later, we will...' it might not have reached such a serious climax. But John unaccountably turned on her.

'I think it would be best for both of us if we separated...'

She stood up, her face pale beneath her make-up. It was a delicately-boned, beautiful face with a soft, vulnerable mouth.

'I'm going home to pack.'

She turned abruptly and walked away from him, threading her way through the crowded tables.

He stood up uncertainly. If they had been at home, he would have called her back – followed her, but already the head waiter was at his elbow.

'You wanted something, sir?'

My wife...

But his lips said:

'Yes, please, my bill.'

Some human beings when they are deeply hurt or afraid turn to a companion for sympathy and understanding. Miranda was of the kind who preferred solitude in which to lick her wounds. She sat on a bench in Green Park hugging her coat round her slim body. It gave some protection from the blustery March wind that was scattering dirty scraps of paper round her fragile evening shoes.

She shivered. The cold seemed to be searching through her clothing into her very soul. She, who had so many gifts from God and man had failed, not once but twice in the basic feminine role of making a husband happy. How? *How?* Why?

When her first marriage had gone on the rocks, she'd sworn to herself it would never happen again. She and David had been so young, so unfitted for the monumental task of marriage and parenthood. The arrival of a baby daughter had proved that neither she nor David had been able to preserve the genuine affection which lay beneath their hot, immature passion, in the face of sordid living conditions, her ill-health and artistic temperament. When the baby died aged six months, from pneumonia, each blamed the other.

'You said we couldn't afford to turn the heating up.'

'If you'd looked after her properly, she'd never have got so ill.'

Now, nearly fifteen years later, she could

see the truth – neither had been to blame except in condemning the other; in trying to assuage grief by hurting the one who could best give comfort.

The divorce had dragged on over three years. During that time, she had met many men but it wasn't until John came into her life she had married again. He was the mature man-of-the-world, utterly dependable where David had been irresponsible; gentle and sensitive where David had been possessive and demanding. John was secure in the family's firm and settled in his way of life; David had been seeking, testing, willing to throw security to the four winds for a mere glimpse of some vague phantom ideal that eluded him.

For a while, the second marriage had been successful. Miranda reminded herself of this, trying to be as unprejudiced as an outsider. Certainly it had been as much of a success as the marriages of most of their friends. There had been minor disputes followed quickly by reconciliations which are part of every marriage. But nothing hurtful – malignant – the way things were tonight. Had she criticised John much over the years? She frowned, trying to search her conscience, knowing there were times when she had felt something lacking in him and had wanted to criticise. *But had she?*

There had been so much to be grateful for

– the beautiful home they shared, the freedom from domestic work, the two cars and a good staff that made life seem smooth and simple; the unlimited dress allowance; the holidays in expensive, exotic places. Materially, John could supply every need and she had never taken his largesse for granted – never could have done so after those years in digs with David... Yet John had said: *'If you feel so dissatisfied with our marriage...'*

Was that the case? Deep, deep down inside, did she feel that to be the truth? The idea of divorce had never once occurred to her, but separation – yes – she had thought of that once or twice. If it were not for John, she would have done so many things!

That's not quite honest, Miranda! she said to herself, her lips taking a grim line. It wasn't something you wanted to do – *but someone you wanted to see.* You wanted to see David again – not for any special reason but just to *see him;* just so you could be absolutely sure you'd done the right thing by divorcing him and marrying John. *If you were free...*

Miranda drew a little Georgian box, which she used as a cigarette case, out of her pocket and then her lighter. After a brief tussle with the wind she managed to light her cigarette. How many times had she tried – and failed – to give it up, she thought dispiritedly! She blew out a cloud of smoke into the frostiness of the early springtime air.

But it wasn't only David – there was Tony, Harry, Patrick, Ludwig, Alastair...

An imposing list! she told herself with harsh sarcasm. *A worthy selection of boy friends – men friends – for any girl.*

Yet she hadn't been the one to make the running – at least not always. They had all fallen in love with her strangely-light, large eyes and shining ash-blonde hair; with her long legs tapering to perfect ankles, and small pointed breasts.

'God gave you more than a fair share of man-appeal,' her mother had said when Miranda was finally of an age to leave school. 'Watch yourself, Mandy – you must learn when to say *"no"* – the men won't!'

Wise mother. Dear, kind, wise Mother, who had died before Miranda's first marriage went adrift. Unashamedly she wept. But for herself she could not weep – neither for herself nor for John nor for a marriage which had begun with such promise and ended after a petty row.

She glanced at her watch. Long past ten o'clock. She shivered, conscious once more of the extreme cold and the absurdity – not to mention the dangers – of staying out here alone in the park when she could be safely at home in her bedroom. Nina, her Spanish maid, would have turned back her bed, switched on her electric blanket, tidied her dressing-table and laid out one of her many

13

beautiful nightdresses. In her mind's eye, Miranda could see the warm golden glow of welcome and yet she did not move from the hard bench seat.

Was it really all over? A marriage broken beyond repair?

If she were to go home now, John would probably be waiting up, worried about her, only too ready for a reconciliation. He would run her bath, fuss over her and later stay all night in her bed, making gentle, considerate love to her...

No! It had gone too far for that. Half of her might long for the security and luxury – for the easy way out – but the proud independent idealist was uppermost. If John had had enough, so, also, had she. Their marriage was not and had never been a true one of the mind and soul; a merging of her being and John's. They had remained always two separate and complete individuals; dependent upon one another for companionship, for sex, for their shared domestic routine, but never for spiritual understanding. There never had existed the kind of love that would dare all, defy all, risk all, *GIVE* all. It was in this way she had loved David and when she had married him she had believed that he loved her just as utterly, as deep-rootedly. Yet they had grown apart, slowly, inexorably as the years passed in the struggle to live. Towards the end, passion alone had drawn them back in the quiet darkness of the night to one another's arms, rebuilding the hot, bright house of physical love on the shifting sands, which inevitably destroyed them.

With the birth of their little girl passion, too, had died; with her death, it had been buried too deep to resuscitate. Love-making with John was completely different; in a way, it had been the same giving of her self, but only outwardly – a physical surrender. It had never been a gift of her innermost self. Was this why she had failed to make John happy? Had he sensed the unconscious reservation?

Wearily, she stubbed out the cigarette. She was too tired now to go on thinking and analysing. She must decide what to do. She could not stay in the Park any longer. A hotel? But she had no luggage. A friend's flat? No, she wouldn't involve her friends. She would *have* to go home and risk running into John.

The smooth gold head lifted. The voluptuous mouth tightened. She was not afraid. She had never been afraid of any man (only of the doctor who had come to tell her poor sweet Melanie was dying). She would go back to the house, tell John she would be leaving in the morning. Nina could help her pack. Maybe by tomorrow some concrete plan would have formulated in a brain that was now too fatigued for rational thought.

She was taken completely by surprise as a

taxi left her at her front door. Within a minute of the cab's departure, John was out beside her, not in a reconciliatory mood but furiously angry.

'Of all the damnably rude ways to behave! What do you think I felt like – the whole restaurant knowing you'd walked out on me – and not knowing where you'd got to? I'm not going to stand any more of it, Miranda…'

'Do stop shouting, John!' Her voice was cold as ice. 'I'm sorry if I embarrassed you – I did not do so deliberately. In the morning I'll pack up and leave.'

Quite suddenly, she knew where she would go – what she must do. John eyed her sullenly as they walked into the house and he closed the door.

'So you did mean it! And exactly where are you going?'

She couldn't tell him. She said:

'Away – somewhere by myself – to think things over. I – I may go abroad. You remember Aunt Alice left me a small legacy. I'll use that.'

But even as she said this, resolve momentarily altered. She remembered the beautiful spring morning when that letter had come. She and John had been breakfasting on the terrace, the bright warm sunshine flashing on the silver coffee-pot and dazzling then with the glittering promise of another beautiful day. Aunt Alice was such a distant relative that news of her death could not touch Miranda to any hypocritical sorrow. The news that she had come into five thousand pounds had meant sheer delight.

'What shall we do with it, darling?'

John had laughed.

'Goodness knows. Put it in the bank, Mandy, until something turns up you really want.'

In those early years of their marriage, she had found it hard to accept John's wealth as hers, too. Not so long before, she and David would have considered five thousand pounds a fortune; a salvation; a solution to all their problems. It could have paid all the bills, supplied David with the paints and canvases he needed; paid for daily help so that she, at last, could begin to write...

To John, it was just a nice but negligible sum to call on when something took her fancy. He'd spent more on the diamond and aquamarine necklace, earrings and ring he had given her for her birthday. He had said, gaily:

'Let's throw a party tonight, a barbecue, to celebrate!'

Perhaps John, too, was remembering, for when he spoke again his voice was quieter as he faced her there in the hall.

'Very well, Miranda. Maybe it's the best thing to do.'

He looked down at his hands, his expression thoughtful.

'What is it you want? I wish I knew! Then, perhaps...' He broke off and his eyes went back to her face, searchingly, as if he hoped to find the answer there.

'Oh, John, if I knew the answer myself ... but all I do know is that we can't go on as we are. We're married and yet ... surely there has to be more to our relationship than the way it is between us? If we loved each other as other couples do ... we are more like friends who sometimes go to bed together.'

John's expression was inscrutable.

'You mean we don't row the way you and David did! No low's, so no high's to follow. Well, that isn't the way I think love should be – a series of hurdles constantly lying in wait to be jumped. It can hurt when you fall Miranda and I don't see the need for men and women to live that way. Maybe you didn't need me as I believed you did. Well, now's your chance to sort yourself out. I've known what I wanted from our marriage but if it isn't what *you* want, then the sooner we both know it the better. I, for one, do not wish to go on with this between us. You're free to go and think things over. Let me have your address in case of emergencies. I'll have a sum paid into your bank account for any other expenses. How long do you think you'll be away?'

'I don't know!' Suddenly there were tears

in her eyes, tears she didn't want him to see. Sheer fatigue, she told herself. Nothing more romantic.

'Shall we say six months? I'll tell our friends you've not been feeling well lately and that the doctors think a prolonged trip abroad is the best thing for you.'

She wanted, then, to say she was sorry – to part from him if not on friendly terms, at least not as a bitter antagonist. But the tears had formed into a lump in her throat. She turned on her heel and left him.

For a long time he stared after her, his eyes unfathomable. Then he bent and patted the head of the cocker spaniel who sat patiently at his feet.

'She'll come back!' he murmured. 'Let her go now, Tess. She'll come back.'

But his voice held no certainty and the doubt in his eyes was at war with the hope in his heart.

She slept fitfully, her mind troubled by incoherent dreams of John and David. At one point she woke exhausted and crying. For a few seconds the memory of one particular dream was frighteningly vivid. David had been making love to her. Their two bodies had throbbed to a mutual rhythm and melody that had been almost too much to bear. Weeping, she had drawn him closer, closer and in the last second before the sharp, breathless climax, she had opened her eyes the better to see the love in his. She saw then that it was John, not David, leaning over her. His face was angry and withdrawn.

'I'm not going to stand any more of it, Miranda.'

In her dream she had been torn by fear at his anger and frustrated by the incompleted act of love.

'I'll go away,' she cried.

'If you'd looked after Melanie properly, she would never have died.'

She struggled in panic, horror, guilt, to get free of this revengeful body towering over her. The desire of a moment ago was chilled now by terror. Then she woke up, trembling and distraught.

She sat up in bed, drenched in sweat, the thin nightgown clinging to her damp body. Tears ran down her cheeks. She could not stop them. She was torn with longing to run through to John's dressing-room, adjoining her own, and feel his arms warm and comforting around her; hear his sensible, level voice reassuring her, telling her that it was only a dream – a nightmare.

But already reality was returning and with it the knowledge that John was inaccessible now.

She glanced at her bedside clock and saw that it was almost five o'clock. She got up and walked into her bathroom and had a quick shower. This room, all her own, had been one of the biggest thrills in the many John's material wealth had given her. To have a bathroom all to oneself – a bathroom suite in palest aquamarine blue – *'the colour of your eyes, darling,'* John had said. The floor was deep-carpeted in crimson and the walls and ceiling were silver. She had spent so many hours in here, warm, relaxed, dreaming, making herself beautiful for John and his guests so that he should be proud of her. It had been so much joy after that sordid, stained little bathroom on the floor below the studio which she and David had had to share with the other tenants...

Stop, mind and thought, stop! she inwardly commanded. *Soon this, too, will be past – I'm going away, going away...*

Back in bed, cool and exhausted, she sought sleep but could not find it.

The doubts of dawn were haunting her. Should she go? Was she throwing away much that was good and worthwhile in this marriage for the sake of a phantom past? Because of some inexplicable urge to return to her young wild passionate love? Suppose the past did not divulge the secret she believed it held – *the secret of her own soul?*

But it will – it must!

I'll see David first – maybe if I can see him again I shall find the answer and perhaps not need to go back any further. Or is this madness

21

– the idiotic whim of a spoilt woman who has too many luxuries and not enough to do?

She saw herself suddenly quite clearly – Miranda Villiers, thirty-three years old, still pretty, still slim enough to pass for twenty-five – her figure a little fuller perhaps but model-fitting. The full sweet mouth which could, when she was happy, turn up at the corners in a wide, embracing smile; could look sulky and petulant, too; the brightness of the big, intelligent eyes was often dulled by boredom. Why hadn't she guessed in time just how bored she'd become once the novelty of being the fabulous Mrs John Villiers had worn off? How utterly meaningless all the parties, the racing at Ascot, the gambling in Cannes, the pointless chatter of other society hostesses, the scandals. Even the theatre, opera and ballet. How utterly useless she was except to look beautiful – like an ornament.

Mrs Woods could run this house without a single order from master or mistress. Nina looked after her clothes. Albert was John's valet. A florist arranged marvellous flowers fresh every three days all over the house. When Miranda left tomorrow, everything would go on just the same – meals would be ordered, delivered, prepared, served and cleared away. Windows would be cleaned; laundry would come and go; the spring-cleaning finished; telephone calls would be made and answered. There was no one, nothing really to reach out a supplicating hand and hold her back; no one but John to say: *'Please don't go, you're needed here.'*

But John had had enough now. Clearly he had outgrown his need of her.

When Nina – a plump, black-browed, smiling Spanish girl, brought in her breakfast-tray, Miranda was so stupefied by fatigue and had such a blinding headache that she could not reply to her maid's customary start to a new day:

'Oh, *Señora – no sol.* Rain again!'

She feigned drowsiness while Nina placed the tray on the bedside table. Through half-closed eyes she watched the girl walk across the thick white rugs to draw back the curtains. What hips the girl had! They swayed under the dirndl skirt, provocatively. Miranda always wondered if Nina had ever had a lover. She sang of love all the time she worked about the house. Rain lashed against the window-panes. The sky beyond was heavy with grey clouds.

Oh, God! thought Miranda. This is no kind of day to go anywhere.

The whole idea of starting a new life seemed unutterably stupid; senseless on a day like this. Even the reason for wanting to go seemed nebulous now and part of a childishly-dramatic tantrum.

Nina had gone to the bathroom. She

23

would be picking up last night's discarded lingerie, tidying up ready for her mistress's morning bath.

'Shall I pour your coffee, *Señora?*'

'No thank you, Nina.'

I shall miss her – my warm, smiling Nina; the born lady's maid, efficient, anticipating my needs, polite yet friendly.

'There's a note from the *Señor.* He said to bring it in with the *Señora's* tray.'

Miranda was suddenly wide awake. Had John, too, regretted last night's decision?

'My dear Mandy,' – it was *Miranda* when he was irritable or cross – *'I don't want us to part with bitterness or ill-feeling. I want you to know I deeply regret things haven't worked out better – perhaps it was partly my fault. Maybe it's just a phase which will pass with the period of separation. I hope so, darling, for I believe there is still something well worth preserving in our marriage ... so long as you believe this, too. But you must be sure.'*

The last words were heavily underlined.

'Please tell Mrs Woods I'll be staying at my Club for the rest of the week. As always
John.'

So he wasn't asking her to change her mind about the separation! Her mouth hardened and the long nervous fingers clenched over the thick notepaper.

'Nina, will you tell Mrs Woods the master

24

is staying at his Club for a few days. I shall be going away, too, so will you come back in half an hour and I'll tell you what I want packed.'

'*Si Señora.*'

How gaily she spoke – understanding nothing, Miranda thought with a grimace as Nina closed the door behind her. But it would be more difficult with Mrs Woods who was a shrewd woman of sixty. She would jump to conclusions – look at her – question her, perhaps.

Maybe Mrs Woods *was* human. Anyhow she would gossip, not to young Nina, but to George.

'Bet madam's had a row with the master. Hope I won't be out of a job because of it. Wonder if there's another man...'

Suddenly Miranda's heart lifted, soared, sang. Last night's resolution was once more sweeping her up, carrying her beyond commonsense to a feeling of freedom, adventure, excitement. She wanted to get out of this well-run, gilded prison of a house. Any moment she chose, she could begin to make enquiries as to David's present whereabouts; perhaps lift the telephone beside her, dial a number and hear his voice.

'I wondered if we could lunch together, David. You know, that little pub in Chelsea we used to go to so often... And we'll be extravagant and order scampi and wine...'

Her breakfast tray untouched, Miranda reached out her hand and lifted the phone.

'I want Directory Enquiries, please.'

Her voice sounded young, expectant, care-free.

CHAPTER TWO

The day for Miranda Villiers was mentally and physically exhausting. By the time the night-train drew out of Kings Cross, she was settled in her first-class sleeper and on the border-line of sleep.

Twelve hours to Aberdeen, she thought drowsily. A long, dull journey. But at least I shall be out of England and I shall see Alastair again.

It was by mere chance that she would be seeing Alastair before any of the others. She had counted on a meeting with David, but although she had obtained his telephone number without difficulty, there had been no reply from his studio. More deeply disappointed than she cared to admit, her first reaction was: I'll go abroad. But John had her passport and she wasn't willing to see him again – not even for her own convenience. She would write to him asking him to post the passport to Aberdeen. Alastair had sounded delighted that he would see her and had urged her to stay as long as she could... She turned her cheek away from the clean cotton pillow-case which seemed unusually rough after her own Irish linen ones at home.

Strange to find Alastair so eager – so submissive, when he spoke to her. In the old days, he'd always been proud, aloof, unwilling to give.

The years rolled back with the roll of the wheels against the railway track – five, ten, fifteen – it was just after she and David had parted finally and she'd felt so terribly alone.

Alastair, too, was alone. He was separated from his wife but because of his two young children there was to be no divorce. He lived in a luxury Park Lane flat, drove a ten-year-old Rolls Royce coupé and always dined at the same epicurean restaurants.

Miranda met him at a dinner-party given by her father. The shared pain of their solitude brought them together, gave them a common interest although after the first brief explanations, neither of them referred to the past. The companionship established at luncheons, dinners, theatres, the ballet, drifted into the beginning of a romance.

At first Miranda was puzzled by the sudden change in his manner. Tall, heavily built and dark-haired, Alastair was a typical Scot; reserved, aloof, introspective, cautious. Telephone calls were never made unless absolutely necessary and then were as brief as possible; flowers he considered a weakness; compliments were rare and given uneasily. But suddenly she became aware that his manner towards her was changing. He became more personal in his attitude and more possessive.

'I do wish you'd give up this Fleet Street job of yours, Miranda.' (He never called her Mandy as David had done). 'Why not take a little cottage in the country, Sussex or somewhere, not too far from Town and devote yourself to your writing.'

Miranda smiled.

'Because in the first place, I couldn't afford to give up my job – still less the rent of a country cottage – and in the second place, I'd be even more lonely in the country than I am in London.'

His eyebrows met in a frown and his usual composure was missing as he said, tacitly:

'I can well afford to rent a cottage for you, Miranda. As for your being lonely, I'd rather hoped I might come down at week-ends...'

If she had not known him so well, she might have thought he was suggesting she should be his mistress. But Alastair was the epitome of convention. It was perfectly true that he could afford the rent of a cottage, without noticing it. The son of a wealthy Scot in the whisky business, he had founded a subsidiary in England and at twenty-eight was very comfortably off.

'At least consider it, Miranda. I don't like to think of you amongst all those journalists – they've absolutely no principles.'

29

Jealousy? Possessiveness? Either emotion was foreign to the Alastair she had known then and gave her the first clue that he was falling in love with her.

She wanted love – badly. She needed a man in her life to make her feel she was necessary – to be needed as a woman both emotionally and physically. But whilst Alastair might well prove an ardent and demanding lover, instinct made her hesitate. She imagined that he might remain aloof and distant even at the ultimate moment of passion. She doubted if she could respond to a man so detached and encased in himself. Only when he discussed his firm, his family, his home in Aberdeen or the Scots, did he become impassioned and at these times she found him attractive. The hazel-green eyes would light up with some inner fire and in more romantic moments of reverie she could picture him striding across the wild Scottish moors to the haunting skirl of bagpipes, fighting some violent battle at the head of his clan.

But would his eyes light up for her, too? Could that fierce Scottish pride and fervour burn in passion for a mere woman?

For many months, she hesitated. On the anniversary of the day she and David had parted, she went away with Alastair for the week-end.

For several months their affair burned like

a wild flame. Afterwards she was able to see those nights for what they were – as the desperate effort to satisfy the physical needs, long denied two highly neurotic individuals. At the time, she was aware of little else but her desire for another meeting, then another. She gloried in his fierce possession of her body; the selfishness of his demands, she saw only as an added expression of his desire for her.

But gradually she realized that it was only her body and not her mind or spirit that he wanted. She must be free for him at all times. He became impatient if she questioned his movements or their next meeting. He spoke often of marriage but would never permit her to bring up the subject of the future – their future.

What finally brought an end to the affair was his heavy drinking. At first she had been unaware of it. It seemed natural that a man in the whisky trade should always have in his home a number of bottles of his own product, and enjoy them. But as her visits to his flat became more frequent during the day as well as in the evenings, she noticed that he was seldom without a glass in his hand. He did not appear particularly affected by it, so she thought at first, but as she got to know him better she saw that it did. He would become a little more dictatorial, a little more aggressive and critical. His good manners grew a trifle blunted as he argued her down with raised voice or swept aside her views with disdainful arrogance.

When she made up her mind to put an end to the relationship, she was totally unprepared for his refusal to accept her decision.

'But I love you, Miranda. No other woman has ever meant as much to me. If it's marriage you want, I'll arrange to divorce Jean. You can't go – I won't let you.'

But she left him all the same, going back to her quiet digs in Hampstead, and to lonely nights and confused memories of a man she believed had cared for her in his strange way – at least, as much as he was capable of doing.

Yet he never tried to contact me – not once from the night I walked out of the flat! Miranda thought sleepily. I suppose that fierce pride of his wouldn't let him belittle himself, not even for the woman he professed to love.

Had he stayed in love all these years or had he found another woman? Someone more submissive – the gentle, uncomplicated 'Yes-girl' whom he really needed. Was it because of her, Miranda, that he had left England to return to his home in Aberdeen or because his father's death necessitated his presence at head office in Scotland?

When the train drew into Aberdeen there was no Alastair waiting eagerly to meet her;

only a car and chauffeur who informed her that a room had been booked for her in a local hotel.

Over a delicious breakfast of strong tea, Scottish bannocks, butter and honey, Miranda reflected wryly that Alastair's failure to meet her and welcome her would have annoyed and hurt her in the old days. Now it merely served to remind her that he was still the same unromantic Scot who would not lower himself to be too sentimental. She spent the morning walking in the wet mist along the sparkling, rushing waters of the River Dee. When she returned to the hotel in time for lunch, Alastair was in the lounge waiting for her.

She recognized him at once, despite the streaks of silver in his hair and the new lines deeply furrowed round his mouth, nose and eyes. He looked extraordinarily tired, even ill, and her intention to be cool and restrained was swept aside at once in concern for him.

'Alistair, are you well?'

He shook hands formally and only the deep penetrating look into her eyes gave away the fact that he was really *glad* to see her again.

'Fine, fine. And you're looking well, Miranda. Take off that wet coat. Let me order you a drink. I've arranged lunch at home at half past one.'

The same dictatorial Alastair taking control with total disregard for her own wishes.

'What will it be – a glass of wine?'

She nodded and watched him move away from her towards the bar. Once she had loved that body, held it to her in a frenzy of desire. Now, she thought ironically, she might be watching the back of a stranger, not exactly alien but with a feeling of complete indifference.

She was shaken out of this by the way Alastair behaved during the next few minutes. She had barely lifted the glass of wine to her mouth before he had finished the large double whisky he had brought himself. The very muscular hand holding the empty glass was shaking. She felt suddenly anxious.

'You're not well!' she said.

He stood up, his face darkening for a moment. She thought he was going to say something violent, even abusive. But after a second he merely excused himself and went quietly back to the bar.

Then she knew. Alastair needed that whisky – must have been needing it pretty badly not to be able to conceal it from her. Now he had started drinking he must have another and he was on the border-line of becoming an alcoholic, she thought with dismay.

He downed his second drink in silence. The moment he had he said abruptly:

'If you've finished, Miranda, we'll push off. My car's outside.'

She found it difficult to make conversation as they drove through the winding roads towards Alastair's ancestral home. In the past he had often described the large stone mansion with its trim well-kept gardens and home farm. Now she saw that the house was in need of paint, the gardens were neglected, fences broken. Everywhere she saw fallen gates, uncut hedges, pathways green with sprouting weeds, flower-beds left to assume a jungle-like growth.

'Bit of a mess!' was his only comment; perhaps the nearest he would come to an apology. 'Thought you'd be more comfortable in a hotel.'

Lunch was served by a dour Scotswoman who looked at Miranda's scarlet nails and pink lipstick with undisguised disapproval. The food, however, was beautifully cooked and despite the fact that Alastair barely touched his meal, Miranda ate heartily. Once or twice she caught his gaze upon her and wished he would say something. He made her feel so strange and uncomfortable.

It wasn't until they were in the study where a log fire blazed in the hearth and coffee was served that he really broke the silence.

'So now you know the worst, Miranda. I suppose you're shocked. Once upon a long time ago, I was shocked, too. Now I don't care – nothing seems to matter much any more except the next drink.'

Compassion warmed and revived her affection for him. She placed her hand on his arm. She said urgently:

'But why? That's what I can't understand, Alastair. Why?'

He shrugged his shoulders with a dejected air, which she found unfamiliar.

'Who can say? I always drank a lot – you used to tell me to cut it down, remember? But in those days, I didn't *have* to. Now I must have it in order to keep going. I don't think there's any excuse. I suppose I'm just a weakling after all.'

Miranda laughed scornfully.

'*You – weak?* I don't believe it. Something has happened...'

His voice was suddenly harsh, his hand now gripped hers like a vice.

'The doctor says it's an illness – a disease. Sometime after you left me, I went back to Jean – thought I might try to patch up our marriage for the sake of the children. I did try, but it just didn't work out. They'd got used to living without me and they all resented my return to the fold as head of the family. Whenever there was a row, I had a few extra drinks to bolster myself up. Jean realized it first, and then the children. They began to despise me and I drank more to forget the look in their eyes.'

'Couldn't your doctor help? There are places for alcoholics.'

He shook his head.

'Only if the patient is willing to help himself. I wouldn't admit to being an alcoholic in those days. Then Jean and the children left me and there didn't seem much point in making the effort, though I did try several times.'

'But you can't go on like this!' Miranda said urgently. 'You don't know how much you've changed, Alastair. You're only forty and you look fifty. If you go on like this, your health will give out altogether.'

'Drinking myself into my grave!' Alastair gave an ironic laugh. 'You sound like my doctor, Miranda.'

She was momentarily silenced. It was not so much the physical as the moral deterioration that appalled her. Alastair had essentially been a strong, determined character – how could he let himself sink into this apathy?

'I nearly ignored your telegram, you know. It came like an accusing voice from the past...'

'Accusing?' she broke in, indignantly.

'I took advantage of your loneliness,' Alastair went on. 'I loved you, Miranda, in my own egotistical way. Yet I made you unhappy. I hated you when you left me – you hurt my pride, you know. Then, when I thought it all over I realized I loved you but I couldn't forgive you for making me see myself as I really was. You did, you know.'

His voice was quiet, even gentle. She felt sudden tears sting her eyelids.

'I'm sorry, really!'

'You need not be. You were the one worthwhile person in my life – but it took me a long while apart from you in order to discover it. By then, you'd married again. So I went back to Jean.'

A log tumbled out with a shower of sparks – the room was softly lit by the firelight and the mood between them sad and reminiscent. Pity seemed to flow through her.

'It wouldn't have worked!' she said sadly. 'I wasn't the kind of woman you needed, Alastair.'

'You've been happy in your second marriage?'

She shook her head.

'I don't seem able to make any man happy for long. Yet all I really asked from life was to be allowed to live it loving one man. I wanted to help him, be a true companion to him as well as a lover.'

Suddenly, without warning, Alastair moved round her and fell on his knees. His hands gripped hers urgently, painfully.

'Stay with me, Miranda. Help me! If you'll help me, I'll try to give up this damned drinking. I'll do what my doctor says – take a cure, anything. I need you. I need your love and your strength. For pity's sake, Miranda, stay with me.'

She was stunned into speechlessness. She did not move. She had once hated this man because he had seemed to have a heart of stone and now he was on his knees to her, *begging.*

'Alastair, please, don't!'

She tried to raise him but he clung to her even more tightly and she felt him trembling the way he used to tremble only in passion; in the darkness, the seclusion of their bedroom.

'You *must* help me – only you can, Miranda. I swear I'll give up the drink. I'll ring the doctor now – you can hear me do it. I'll promise to let him treat me, Miranda.'

I can't, she thought, frightened by the rising hysteria in Alastair's voice – the increasing loss of control. I don't love him. I don't feel anything but pity.

Yet, something else moved in her too – a tiny spark of satisfaction that here was a man who needed her – who could give her life some meaning and purpose. They had been lovers once – when he grew well again they might reach a new, more understanding relationship.

As if sensing her hesitation, he renewed his appeal. Suddenly, he stood up and walked away from her into the hall. When he returned, his ashen face had more colour and his hands were steadier. He held a glass of whisky which had been only half consumed.

'My doctor is coming over this evening to meet you,' he said eagerly. 'See, Miranda, how much good you've done me just by being here. I can leave this on the table...' he pointed to the glass '... and because of you I don't have to finish it. I won't even touch it unless you say I can.'

He was almost jubilant, almost the old Alastair, full of self-confidence and as always taking it for granted she would do as he wished.

'You'll like Dr Garth. He's been our family doctor for years. He'd almost given me up as a bad job but it'll all be different when he hears you're willing to stay and help me.'

'Alastair, I didn't promise anything. I don't think it would be possible. You mustn't count on me for anything...'

He seemed deaf to her protests. He went on talking enthusiastically about the future. He'd have the garden put in order, the house painted, the drive re-surfaced. Miranda could redecorate to her own wishes.

'I've plenty of money,' he told her. 'You see, I sold the firm – hardly seemed worth keeping it on – and I'm living on the capital.'

By tea-time, Miranda felt as if she was being pressurized by a steam-roller. She could no longer think coherently and her mind became a confusion of conflicting issues. Alastair seemed to take it for granted she would stay. His very certainty was tending to threaten her composure – her logical reasoning that if she did what he wanted it would be madness. She was frightened *of* him and *for* him. Most of all she was frightened of her growing concern for his welfare.

A further shock awaited her. Dr Garth came. He insisted upon Alastair absenting himself while he talked to Miranda. When Alastair had reluctantly left them alone, the elderly doctor spoke bluntly:

'The puir chap told me on the telephone you might be willing to stay and look after him. Obviously you don't realize that he's beyond a cure. He's been drinking himself to death, ruining his liver and his kidneys, for the past six years. He may last another year but I myself doubt if it'll be beyond Christmas. There isn't a thing you can do for him. I'm sorry.'

'You mean he's *dying?*'

'Exactly!'

'And he doesn't know it?'

'I've told him, but he refuses to accept it. Deep down he knows – when he's sober. But those occasions are so rare, he's usually unaware of the truth.'

'But he's sober now. He has only had a double whisky since lunch…'

41

'Och, no, my dear – he'll have been through at least two bottles today. He drinks alone in his bedroom. Once an alcoholic reaches this stage, he can't do without it – like a drug addict. Possibly for your sake he'd make the effort – today he's tried to conceal his drinking, but usually when he's alone, he just sits with the bottle until Mrs McQuire puts him to bed.'

Miranda's fingers felt icy-cold. It was as though she'd been slapped in the face.

'I'm sorry, Mrs…' the doctor paused and looked at her with professional concern. 'No doubt this has come as a shock, but you should know the truth before you become further involved. My advice to you is to go back to England and forget you ever saw puir Alastair. You can't help him.'

'But he begged me – he seems to feel I could help.'

'Listen to me, my dear; today he has made a supreme effort to appear normal – he couldn't keep it up. By tomorrow he'll be dead drunk again – possibly beyond recognizing you or even caring whether you're alive or dead. Maybe by tonight it'll happen. The whisky is the only thing that can give him relief. Do you understand? He's beyond the help of anyone unless he consents to go into a clinic, which he refuses to do.'

She was glad to be alone for a while after the doctor left; alone, to try and gather her strength to say good-bye to Alastair. It would need all her courage to deliver what she felt would be the *coup de grâce*.

But as the clock ticked away the minutes, she felt her courage deserting her. She looked up quickly as the door opened. It was Mrs McQuire who came in, her face expressionless.

'The Master is indisposed, and I've taken the liberty of ordering a taxi to take you to your hotel.'

Miranda stood up, words failing her.

'The Master won't be coming down again today,' Mrs McQuire said firmly. 'Maybe the doctor told you he's a very sick man. They give him six months at the most. There isn't anything you can do for him, Mistress.'

Miranda stood up. She felt sick, deflated, like a rudderless ship fighting an impossible storm, buffeted – even broken. One half of her mind accepted the facts – the other, the part which had known Alastair before he'd given way to his addiction, still insisted this was all a nightmare.

That night in bed, she cried herself to sleep. She wept over the ruin of a good man and (without knowing it) out of an undeniable relief because she had not after all married such a man. She even muttered a painful prayer that when she found David, the image of their love would not likewise crumble into dust.

CHAPTER THREE

As she sat in Ludwig's Paris apartment waiting for him to return from a luncheon engagement, Miranda realized that she had not by any means recovered fully from the shock of discovering that Alastair was an alcoholic. She was still shaken by the dreadful change time had wrought in him. She was no longer sure that this sentimental journey into the past was a good idea. Had it not been for her reluctance either to return home to John or to make the effort to start a new life on her own, she might have given up trying to find herself – her real self – amongst the ashes of burned-out passions.

She lit a second cigarette in order to give her restless fingers some occupation and leaned her head against the back of a beautiful Louis XVI walnut and gilt chair with *gros-point* tapestry. She liked French furniture of this period. She had hoped after leaving Aberdeen that she might find that David had returned to his studio, but a neighbour living on the opposite side of the Mews had leaned out of a window to inform her that he was away, had gone to America, she thought – irrevocably dashing Miranda's hopes. The only other information she had been able to extract was that the neighbour thought he would be back in three weeks, but about this she was uncertain.

The thought suddenly struck Miranda that the reason why she was looking up Ludwig Strupner before Patrick was because he bore several points of resemblance to David. Ludwig, too, was a good artist. Ludwig as a painter shared David's eye for all that was beautiful. Both men, because of this approach to life, so often saw life through the same concentrating, critical lens. Strange that she had not realized during those months when she had been Ludwig's mistress that this kinship with David was one of the things that had drawn her to him.

She looked with curiosity round Ludwig's beautiful salon. Walls panelled with striped grey silk; Aubusson carpet; the delicate Louis XVI furniture; the rich mulberry satin curtains; the studded velvet sofas; the exquisite paintings and collection of priceless ivories which he had brought back after a trip to China. All were still here. Nothing was changed. Time seemed to have stood still. She alone, so she felt, could show proof that twelve years had passed since Ludwig first brought her here.

She drew out a powder compact from her bag and studied her face in the mirror. There were faint lines round her eyes; the barest slackening of the muscles under the skin of her throat. Would Ludwig, who had idolised the face of the young girl he had known, be disappointed in the woman?

Her mind sped backwards across the years to her childhood. In those days, Ludwig was one of her father's friends and contemporaries – a handsome, dark-haired, distinguished-looking man with a high forehead, prominent cheekbones and long, tapering fingers. He would come to dinner with her father wearing a black overcoat lined with wild mink and collared with astrakhan. Sometimes, if it were Bessie's night out, her father would permit her to hang up this coat and Ludwig would rest his hand on her long fair hair and smile at her, and murmur his thanks. Once, when her father had brought him up to say goodnight to her, she had been fascinated by the bottle-green smoking jacket Ludwig was wearing.

'It's such a pretty colour,' she said, sleepily. 'My father's dinner-jackets are always black and that's dull.'

She remembered that particular evening as a kind of landmark, for Ludwig had noted then her own appreciation of colour and beauty so he had begun to take an interest in her. Her mother was typical of the well-to-do parent of her day. She led a busy social life, relegating Miranda to the care of a nurse and then a series of governesses until she was of an age to be sent to boarding school. Her father, too, saw little of his young daughter and until the advent of Ludwig, no grown-up had ever taken much interest in Miranda unless it were to comment upon her clothes, her behaviour, her health or her education. She had grown to love Ludwig as any small girl will love a doting uncle. He took her round the London art galleries explaining the works of the great Masters in words which often she could not understand. He took her to concerts and to the opera, and if at times she fell asleep in the middle of them, he was never cross but chided himself for keeping her up so late. In her teens, however, she saw less of him because she was so often away at school. Occasionally in the holidays he would come over from Paris where he was then living and take her out for the day.

Somehow, with Ludwig, she could be relaxed and at ease. The awkward, adolescent gawkiness which overcame her in the presence of her parents or their ordinary friends was strangely absent in Ludwig's company. Often she would find herself wishing, guiltily, that he were her father and that when she left school she could go to live with him in his beautiful Paris flat which he had described to her in some detail.

There was one wonderful summer. The year before she met David, Ludwig had rented a small studio in London so as to be able to paint the portrait of a business magnate who had recently been knighted. As the client could spare so little time for sittings, most of the portrait was painted in his absence. Ludwig allowed Miranda to stand at his side watching with fascination every moment of his brush, the skilful blending of paints – the slow, incredible but definite emergence of a man's face and form beginning to come to life and breathe on the flat canvas.

Ludwig's black hair was turning grey and he was forced to wear horn-rim spectacles for close work, but he remained the handsome idol of her childhood until the last day of the holidays when she had met David, one of Ludwig's young student painters and protégés. From that moment, she had had eyes for no one else, time for no one else, no love to spare for any other man. A year later, she and David were married. She had not even noticed that Ludwig was not at the wedding.

She hadn't seen Ludwig again until she had run into him quite by chance in Rules. She was trying at that time to pick up the threads of her journalistic career after reaching the decision to break finally with Alastair. Ludwig was lunching at the next table with the Art Editor of one of the national dailies. He stood up and waved to her. She rushed over to him and within minutes they were talking easily and with pleasure. She had at once accepted his invitation to dine.

'I still have the same studio, Mandy,' he told her with the old charming, slow smile. 'Perhaps you would like to come round about seven. I have a portrait I would particularly like you to see.'

Once there, she had been both surprised and flattered to find the portrait was of herself.

'I did it after you had deserted me to marry your David,' he said, handing her a drink, and looking down at her appraisingly.

She stared at the soft rich tones of the portrait and wondered if that lovely eager face was really her own.

'You've made me look beautiful. If only I *really* looked like that!'

He stared at it.

'At the time, Mandy, you looked exactly like this. It took me many weeks to portray the radiance which glowed from you. Now...' he paused, thoughtfully and looked back at her. 'Now it is not so like you, perhaps. There is sadness in your face and a little bitterness.'

Suddenly she was in tears. Her face was hidden against his shoulder. His arms were firm and comforting, holding her tightly. Until this moment, she had not been able to talk to anyone of the disastrous break-up of

49

her marriage, nor of the agony she had suffered when her baby died. Ludwig was the one person in the world in whom she could confide.

He had said nothing but continued to rock her gently in his arms until she gained control of herself. Then he had put a finger beneath her chin, tilting her wet sad face so that she was forced to look up at him. He had said, quietly, astoundingly:

'I love you, my dear. I love you, my dear, dear Mandy.'

Surprise robbed her of speech. She had continued to stare at him unbelievingly.

The tenderness in his eyes gave way to irony. He let her go and turned from her.

'I suppose this seems ridiculous to you. I must seem very old indeed to your young eyes.'

She had never before thought about his age. He was just, well – just Ludwig. Certainly she had never thought of him as a woman thinks of a man in whom she might become interested sexually. He had been in a special category of his own, rather the way she might say: 'So-and-so is not a man. He is my brother.'

Ludwig was someone wise and kind and companionable. *Dependable*, all-knowing, a mixture of parent, uncle, friend. Now, suddenly, she saw him as himself. At fifty-two, he was not old but neither was he young as

David had been. It was possible to believe that he was more handsome in the late prime of his life than he might have been as a very young man. With his aesthetic, ivory-hued face, and long thin nose and delicate mouth, he looked like a distinguished poet or musician. Success as a painter had given him immense self-assurance. His early childhood in his native Austria had endowed him with a facile, Continental charm, always immensely attractive to women. In a sense, he was ageless.

'You do not seem old to me, Ludwig,' she said at last. As if these words were like a key to unlock the door of restraint, suddenly she was in his embrace again, only this time he was kissing her eyes, her lips, her throat with all the passion of a man deeply in love. She seemed suddenly to have no will of her own. So totally unprepared had she been for this astounding new side to Ludwig, she could not make up her mind whether she should put an end to his caresses.

'I love you, I love you,' he kept saying against her ear. 'I've loved you since you were a tiny girl. I was waiting for you to grow up, Mandy, waiting for you to leave school and become a woman so that I could tell you just how much I loved you. And then, before I had a chance, you met David and I thought you were lost to me for all time. For months I couldn't paint. I'd lost not only you, but all

51

my inspiration. Then suddenly, I felt a burning need to have you back with me, if not in flesh then in likeness. I began to paint that portrait and with it came some release from the torment of loneliness which haunted me after your marriage. I've loved many women, but not one in the way I've loved you, my dearest.'

She felt herself responding to the flattery underlying those words. Here was her hero, her idol, at her feet. Here was one of the world's best-known artists offering her his love and his adoration when he could have had any of the world's most beautiful women at *his* feet. For David had told her how besieged Ludwig had been by many famous and beautiful women. But it was her, Miranda, whom he wanted.

He drew her down beside him on to a couch spread with a white fur rug. The last light had faded. The studio was in deep shadow. He reached out his hand to unfasten the velvet dress from her white shoulder. She felt a moment of fear, or was it reluctance? It was David who should be bending over her – David to whom her body belonged. But then, as Ludwig's experienced hands moved gently over her body it didn't seem to matter any more. It was as if her will as well as her body were completely subjugated to his and she surrendered with a passion that matched his own.

The next morning, Miranda awoke from a deep sleep to a feeling of unreality, as she tried to sort out her confused emotions. The morning post arrived followed by a florist's girl with a cellophane box of pure white roses.

When they had parted last night, Ludwig told her that he was leaving next day for Paris and had begged her to go with him. He had argued fiercely against her first impulsive refusal.

'I'm not asking you to have a sordid little affair with me, Mandy. I want to marry you. As soon as your divorce comes through, I want to make you my wife. I'm a wealthy man. I can give you anything in the world you want. I will live where you please, as you please. I ask nothing but the right to love you. I do not even expect your complete love in return. It is enough that we should be married.'

It would have been so easy to say 'yes'. Her life was pointless, without direction, and she craved stability. Yet she could not give him that answer until the next morning.

Miranda was unable to find any one reason for her hesitation in accepting Ludwig's proposal. She didn't love him – at least, not in the way she had loved David. What she once felt for Ludwig had been a child's adoration which, suddenly, had become hopelessly confused by the urgency of physical passion. Before they had grown apart, she had shared with David a wild, mutual delight in each others' bodies. But he had never aroused in her the same depth of sensual desire and satisfaction that she had experienced in Ludwig's arms. He was a marvellous lover. She was a little frightened. One half of her wished that they could return to the comfortable platonic friendship of her childhood days. The other half longed perversely for a repetition of the wild ecstasy which Ludwig alone had roused in her.

She dressed slowly and wandered restlessly round her room. Again and again her eyes turned to the flawless white roses that Ludwig had sent to her. What was holding her back? She always appreciated his brilliant company; they had never argued or quarrelled. He understood her as no one else in the world and knew more about her even than David.

David, *David!* She knew then that despite all the bitterness and unhappiness deep within her she still loved *him.* She knew, too, that there was no hope for their marriage. Love, after all, was not enough when all else failed and she could not stand the violent rows, the bitterness and, worst of all, the cool disinterest that had developed in David's eyes when he looked at her.

Had they been too young for marriage? It

was quite impossible to believe that Ludwig would ever have behaved with David's cruel egotism. He was surely sensitive and gentle where David was blind and cruel. She would be safe with Ludwig and yet ... and yet...

A week later, she flew to Paris and to Ludwig. How magnificently he had made her welcome! He tried never to let her regret her decision to join him. In the daytime, he painted with renewed vigour and enthusiasm, telling her that she had inspired him to his finest work. At night they would put records on the stereo which she saw now, still standing against the wall not far from the Bechstein piano. He loved to play that piano and was no mean musician. Sometimes, he read to her – a volume of Russian essays; Voltaire's *Candide,* poems by Voltaire, essays of Anatole France. Occasionally he would hold a musical evening when great artists sang while he accompanied them. At night, he made love to her with the passionate relentless intensity of a man who knows that this is probably his last love as well as the greatest.

He lavished presents on her – paintings, beautiful-bound books, exquisite pieces of antique jewellery, expensive furs and always, always white roses. He never tired of painting her, sometimes in evening dress, sometimes casually in slacks and heavy sweaters, often in the nude. She began to take the same pride as he did, in the fine lines of her delicate body. Sometimes, in the cold early hours of dawn, she would lie awake and try to give a name to her feelings for this man; this great artist. She was infatuated with him and by him and by the life they led, yet she could never quite believe in the love he so often begged her to express. Her body and mind were enslaved by him and yet her heart remained curiously, determinedly aloof...

As the months passed, she began to feel an increasing restlessness. It was as if after those years of desperate hard work and poverty with David, this enclosed luxurious life of the complete Sybarite with Ludwig was beginning to stifle her. She was still young. She felt the need of other young society. But she and Ludwig seldom went out with friends and although no mention was made of it, she knew they were both a little embarrassed by the great difference in their ages.

Ludwig assured her that he was entirely happy. He spoiled her whenever it was possible to do so and once or twice she found herself taking advantage of his goodness and becoming irritable or short with him for no better reason than to give their relationship a momentary jolt. She would find herself longing for the relief of a good quarrel, to be followed by the stimulus of a reconciliation. But there was never any cause to quarrel with Ludwig who lived only to please her. She began to see that the time would come when she must escape. She would make up her mind that when his next portrait of her was complete, she would go; making the break as kind and gentle as was possible, perhaps by saying she wished to take a short holiday alone in England – then prolonging it until he was forced to realize that she did not intend to return. But almost as if he sensed her intention, he would claim her again through the passionate delight of their physical union. Her resolve would weaken as she looked into those fine dark eyes of his, so full of worship for her. His love amounted to idolatry. Her body had become a shrine at which he knelt – as exalted a devotee as any mystic acolyte. She had only to see that haunting, intellectual face transfigured and grown youthful through desire for her, to know that she was lost again. As a lover he was almost irresistible.

Strangely enough, it was Ludwig who broke the dream and forced the final parting. He was called to America at twenty-four hours notice and could not take her with him. They spent their last night together in the studio. Ludwig wanted to finish a miniature of Miranda on ivory so that he could take it with him. He worked through the night and as dawn broke they slept for a few hours in one another's arms. Now that the moment had come to part, she couldn't bear him to leave. Her cheeks were wet with tears as she slept in his arms for the last time. Exhausted by the long night and too much emotion, she never heard him go. When she woke, the house was silent. On her pillow was a single white rose pinned with a fabulous emerald brooch.

The Miranda of twelve years later glanced at her watch. She saw that it was nearly three o'clock. Surely Ludwig would be home from lunch at any moment. She had given him no warning. Had she told him she was coming back to see him after all these years, would he have rushed home to her or did he hate her for her betrayal? When he had gone to America she had meant to join him as soon as possible, but once out of his presence the spell broke. Her first desolate loneliness was replaced by a relief which she tried to stamp on, as a disloyalty to the man who had loved her so unselfishly and devotedly all her life. But as his absence dragged from days to weeks, she knew that whatever link had existed between them was broken at last.

She was offered a job on a small provincial newspaper and returned to London. She left no forwarding address for Ludwig's letters, feeling that she must at all costs be firm in her resolve to break with him completely lest he should fly home and try to recall and reclaim her. In a farewell letter to him she tried to express her gratitude and to make him understand that although her departure might make him unhappy, she would eventually hurt him more if she stayed.

Had he understood? She felt that he must have done so, partly because he had always been sensitive to her feelings, and partly because he had made no effort as time went by to get in touch with her.

Looking back over the years she could appreciate now how cruelly she must have hurt him. Perhaps one of her main reasons for wishing to see him now was to reassure herself that he had found peace of mind and contentment towards the end of his life. How old would he be now? In his late sixties. Had the years treated him kindly?

The door opened suddenly, startling her. He came into the room. The familiar, charming voice with only the faintest trace of an accent said:

'Mandy, I couldn't believe it when my man said it was you. How are you, my dear?'

He had aged. His hair was quite white now and he stooped a little. But he was still handsome. Her first reaction was one of immense pleasure in seeing him again. Her second, more critical glance gave her a slight shock. The lover who had seemed ageless, was now an old man.

He stood silently, looking down at her with a half-smile – with the intent, searching gaze of the artist as well as the man.

'You are as beautiful as ever but your eyes are sad. Tell me about yourself. What brings you to Paris?'

He sat down opposite her. His movements were slow and showed the slight stiffness of old age.

Uneasily, Miranda noted this tragic change in his physical being brought about by time, and it depressed her unutterably.

'I came to see you!' she said and felt the sting of tears behind her eyelids.

He gave that quaint, quizzical smile and followed it with a deep bow.

'I am honoured, my dear.' There was no sarcasm in his voice. He waited then in silence for her to explain herself more fully.

'I – I think I wanted to say I'm sorry!' Miranda blurted out the apology with a childish abruptness she could not restrain.

Once this man had helped to give her a sense of maturity – a woman's poise and confidence in herself. Now, in this moment of truth, she felt like a child again, gauche and ill at ease.

He shook his head at her.

'But there is no need for you to be sorry!' His voice was gentle with all its old charm.

'You gave me one wonderful year, my dear. For that I was grateful, even in the first agony of our separation. It will not make me happy to hear you yourself ever regretted the step you took.'

'Oh, Ludwig!' The exclamation broke from her uneasily. She might have felt better if he had accused her of cruelty in the past, or selfishness, ingratitude after his great love and many, many kindnesses.

He reached out a hand and placed it over hers. She saw with surprise that it was heavily veined and fragile – it showed his age more than his face or his slight stoop had done. She was reminded of those exquisite ivories which he had always liked and collected.

'There is no need for remorse. I knew all along it must one day happen that way. It was hard when it came – the finality of it, but perhaps it was for the best. I do not think I could have stood a scene of farewell and torn myself away from you.' He sighed and closed his eyes as though to shut out a vision of pain.

'Did you know I would leave you?' she asked, surprised.

'But of course. You were never in love with me, my dear. It was on your part an infatuation – a need for my strength and tenderness – no more. You were never quite all mine.'

The painful tears welled over now. She

hastily wiped them away.

'I wish I could have loved you – the way you deserved, Ludwig.'

'No, Mandy! You were not meant for an old man's pleasure. I stole that year from you and you made me so very happy. It was as though life gave me something very precious and adorable – on loan – then asked for it back. I ought not to complain. Tell me, now, what has happened to you since the parting of our ways?'

She sat silent a moment. Her gaze kept wandering restlessly round the salon picking out each beautiful, familiar *objet d'art*. She had an uncanny sensation that she had never left Ludwig and that he had just returned home from a visit to an art gallery or one of those walks he used to enjoy in the *Bois;* that he was the Ludwig of twelve years ago – tall, erect, so young compared with this tired old gentleman. He would hold out his arms to her. She would run to him and feel the wine of an intoxicating passion flow through her veins in response to his kiss. He would touch her hair and murmur:

'My lovely, lovely Mandy – my beautiful child! *Ma chère enfant!*'

Often he had used that French endearment.

Today she was no child, she thought bitterly. She, too, had aged though her years were as nothing compared with his. Yet she

62

felt the shivering touch of autumn – no, of *winter* for Ludwig; ice-cold and remorseless following its normal cycle, bringing in its trail the dry dead swirl of leaves and the sad whine of the wind. Oh, how terribly sad it was to grow old! She would have wished that Ludwig of all men could have remained alert and agile, on the crest of the wave before it tumbled and washed him downwards with such relentless force.

And what of the lost opportunities? She might have said that she had always taken the chances life had held out to her. In some measure it was so. But she had been chasing the Blue Bird of happiness – and always in vain – always to be disappointed or frustrated as though her passion died upon a kiss.

Here in this very room, in the old days, she would sit sometimes with Ludwig while he read poems to her; poems in French and in German which he translated if she did not understand; poems in English. He was a great lover of English verse; a few lines from this book, a few from that...

Rupert Brooke had appealed to him, she remembered; that sad yet humorous, innocent yet cynical, young man who had died for his country in the full glory of his golden youth.

'I dreamt I was in love again
With the One Before the Last...'

She quoted that to herself uneasily, almost ashamedly because the words so perfectly fitted her. Whom had she ever *really*, steadfastly loved? Only David. Why must she always discover some flaw that appeared all too soon in what once seemed perfection?

How could she tell Ludwig about the others? The One Before the Last... *Oh, God,* she thought. *Which one?*

'You are distressing yourself, my dear,' said Ludwig in a quiet, compelling voice. 'I can see it in your eyes.'

'You were always able to see,' she sighed.

'Don't tell me anything if you don't want to, my dear.'

She said with difficulty:

'You knew that I married again – or perhaps you did not hear?'

'No, I did not,' he said, quietly.

'Well ... there were others – never mind their names,' she said painfully, 'and for a while with each one I thought I had found permanent happiness. In particular I believed that to be so when I married John.'

'John?'

'My husband whom I've just left.'

Ludwig's eyes narrowed, twinkling into the most tender of smiles.

'Poor John!'

'Yes, pity him if you like. Never me! I'm the one who should not be pitied, for I'm sure it's always my fault. There is something in me, Ludwig, that nothing can satisfy. I don't mean the physical me, but that other side. I came so near to absolute happiness at first with David. Perhaps it was the real thing and I did not appreciate it then. Who knows? Yet John is a wonderful man. I was happy with *him*...'

She broke off again. She did not want to be wholly disloyal to John, yet she longed to go on confiding in Ludwig – the way she used to do as a child, as a young girl. He had always been able to advise and help her. He had such infinite wisdom and understanding of life.

'But this love with John was never as good as it used to be with David?' he asked, watching her.

She should not have been surprised at the accuracy of the construction he had put upon the matter. Who knew her better than Ludwig? What man alive was more sensitive to the swift fluctuating moods of a woman's heart?

'No,' she whispered. 'It was never right.' She had never loved John with the same wild joy and complete abandon that she had felt for David. Then she added with an honesty Ludwig had always admired in her:

'Neither was the physical side as glorious – as perfect as it was with *us*, Ludwig.'

'So you did miss me – a little!'

His smile was proud as well as sad and his shoulders seemed to straighten to a semblance of his lost vital youth.

'A great deal.' She smiled back at him.

'But your memories of me, I hope, were never the cause of your unhappiness. I can see you are confused, Mandy.'

'True. John and I quarrelled – nothing serious but we just did not understand one another. I could never quite give all of myself to him and he obviously felt that I was not a good wife to him. When we separated, I felt I must have time to sort myself out. I felt that the years were slipping by and I was wasting them. Life is wasted when one does not really love.'

'So it was with me!' he said, and sighed deeply. 'I have some sympathy with your John, for you see I have known what it is to love a person who was never quite my own. It can be torture. So you have run away again my dear, dear Mandy?'

He held out a hand to her.

Suddenly she was at his feet, her head on his knees. She felt those well-remembered fingers – full of tenderness – softly stroking her hair.

'Help me, Ludwig,' she whispered. 'What should I do? Ought I to go back to him and try again? Or would we be happier apart? Materially, I have everything I want – John spoiled me – just as you did. Yet it isn't enough and I know *he* isn't happy.'

'And David?'

'David? I haven't seen him since we parted all those years ago. I – I tried to get in touch after I separated from John but he was away.'

'I think you should see David again before you make up your mind what to do about your husband. You see, I am of the belief that you still love David. I know when you first came to me you thought you hated him, but there is truth in the saying that hate is akin to love. You were never indifferent to David. He had power to move you deeply. You were hurt by him; bitter, despairing, angry ... but never indifferent.'

She knew that Ludwig, as ever, had spoken the truth.

They sat in silence which was broken finally by Ludwig.

'You must stay to tea with me, Mandy. I'd like to show you my latest paintings. There is one I want to give you – as a souvenir of the past. I painted it for you soon after you left me. I always hoped that one day I would be given a chance to present it to you. Will you give me that pleasure?'

She could see that it would mean much to him if she accepted his present. He rang the bell for the valet to bring tea, then came back to Miranda, took her hand and walked with her up to the studio – the fine long room with its north light – running right over the top floor of the house.

She felt an extraordinary sensation that time itself moved backwards instead of forwards – so often had she come into this studio with him and watched him paint, or posed for him. Below the long window lay Paris – the Left Bank – the waters of the Seine flowing through the most beautiful city in the world. Here, she had almost found that elusive perfection. *Almost* ... not quite.

It was the old eager Ludwig who drew the canvas out of a pile of others, fixed it on an easel, then taking her arm, stood beside her while she looked at it.

At first the painting was a shock. It was unlike anything Ludwig had done before; no conventional portrait this, but an artist's impression bearing all the magnificence and symbolism of classic inspiration. For a moment the subject confused her; she even found it sinister, although she was at once delighted by the richness of the colours and the original design.

A young slave-girl, wearing a short white tunic was spreadeagled against a tree. The girl was *herself;* herself when young – as she must have appeared to Ludwig who had known her then. It was a staggering work. It took Miranda some time to pick out all the details and to understand the artist's meaning.

The face, the tall slender body, the curved outstretched arms with the long pointed fingers were undeniably Miranda's. She could not fail to recognize herself. But what did it mean – this curious crucifixion? The girl was straining forward as though struggling against the thongs that tied her wrists to the branches. There was a suggestion of strong wind, for her fair hair streamed out behind her and had become entangled in the twigs of the leafless tree. On her face there lay a look of anguish and of appeal; yet the whole poise suggested hope and expectancy – and a desperate desire for freedom.

Ludwig remained silent. Miranda, more intellectually moved than she had been for years, continued to examine the canvas. Now she could discern the outline of hills shrouded in deep blue mist, stretching away to the right of the canvas. But what interested her immensely were two figures emerging from the shadows in the background. One of a man – beautiful, vigorous, wearing like herself a tunic that suggested Ancient Rome. Hand in hand with him was a small naked curly-headed child. Their backs were turned as though they were about to walk away but their two faces looked over their shoulders. Both man and child wore expressions of entreaty – and seemed as though they were reluctant to abandon her. The symbolism – the significance surrounding her own spiritual enslavement fascinated her.

When she turned to Ludwig, she found it difficult to speak. At last she said:

'Who are they – those two figures, Ludwig? Whom do they represent?'

He pressed her arm against his side. He could feel her trembling.

'You like the painting?'

'Yes, yes, it's marvellous. The finest thing you have ever done. I can understand most of it. It is myself – crucified by my own passions, tortured by my indecisions and uncertainties. Yes, I see that part of it. But who are *they* – the man and the child?'

'David, perhaps, and the little one who should have lived. Or is it some other man to whom you belonged? I leave you to interpret that as you wish.'

She remained inarticulate. She could not drag her gaze away from the canvas. Somehow it filled her with a sense of deep grief and even despair.

Ludwig spoke again.

'The man is certainly not meant to be *me*. For I knew, even when you were still with me, that you were not mine and that whatever I gave you it was never a sense of complete freedom. I hoped when I saw you again, an hour ago, that you had burst your bonds and that your anguish was over. Now I am not sure, my poor darling.'

'Oh, Ludwig,' she said, helplessly.

70

'Please take the painting,' he said. 'I want you to have it. There was something about you which I felt deeply and which I had to express in my art. The painting was meant always for you. *I* need no outward picture of your face. If I were blind I would still be able to see it. You have always been in my heart and you always will be. The privilege of having loved you, Miranda, and possessed you for a time at least, puts me in your debt for ever.'

'I don't deserve this,' she said, choking, and hid her face in her hands.

'My dear, my dear, whatever I do I must not make you sad. Is it not some little comfort to you to know that I still love you?'

'I don't deserve this,' she repeated and caught the hand that had created this great painting. Turning from the sight of the slave-girl's anguish, she put Ludwig's ivory hand against her wet cheek and sobbed. He kissed her hair then her eyes but there was no passion between them. That, she knew was finished. Her body could never again take fire from his touch, nor would her heart beat in furious anticipation of the embraces, the caresses that once had transported them both up here in this very studio; with the roar of Paris drifting up to them through the open windows.

'Come, my dear,' he said. 'Tea will be ready. Do you remember how we both loved our Russian tea with lemon in it? I used to love watching the beauty of your hands as you lifted my silver teapot and poured my tea. I loved everything about you.'

'Why, why did I ever leave you, Ludwig?' The question was torn from her.

'Because,' he said as they walked downstairs, 'I was no more right for you than the others have been. But you must not cry. Sometimes it is sad and even dangerous to dig among the ashes of a lost love and try to rekindle it. Let us face the future – forget our sorrows. As you may remember, I have always been a fatalist. What is to be – is to be. We cannot fight destiny.'

'I don't want to think that,' she cried. 'I don't want to feel that everything is mapped out, and that we're helpless to prevent it.'

'Still the same eager, enthusiastic, strong-willed, independent Miranda,' he laughed softly. 'I can see you have not changed and I am glad you, at least, have not lost your fire. Always a phoenix will rise from the ashes for you, my dear. Always you will search for the ultimate, unwilling to accept second-best. But one day you will realize what to me has become an absorbing truth – that it is not old age which is hard to live with but youth. Agonized youth stretching out its hands, refusing to believe that everything passes, even love and life itself.'

'You make me feel so ashamed of myself,'

she whispered.

'That is the last thing I want. A beautiful, passionate, generous woman like yourself should never be ashamed. Shame belongs only to the ungenerous – the frigid – the cowards who even when they are offered a great love are too niggardly to accept it in case they should have to pay too high a price.'

She stayed with him until late that evening. Even with her restlessness of heart and her uncertainty, she experienced a deep satisfaction in the renewal of her friendship with Ludwig. It seemed when the time came for her to leave that they were closer together in mind, now, than they had ever been when they were lovers.

He became once more the interesting, intriguing Ludwig with his countless stories of his famous, talented colleagues and friends.

'An art dealer I know is building a new salon, with many windows looking across to the Bay of Naples. He wishes me to paint a fresco for the walls. It will take me many months, perhaps years. So as I slip further into old age I shall have something to interest and satisfy me.'

'May you always be happy, my dear, dear Ludwig, for you deserve it,' Miranda said and was still the little girl of long ago, sitting at his feet.

When they parted he gave her a bunch of

white roses. They looked pure, exquisitely fresh, lying among the dark green leaves under their veil of cellophane. He had sent his man out to buy them. The love and sentiment behind the gesture touched her deeply. She promised to write – to keep in close touch with him from now onward. He promised to send the painting to her the moment she sent him her address.

He watched her go with the white roses in her arms. He thought:

'Like a bride ... poor, sweet Miranda. She will always be like a bride – always there will be the untouched virgin in her – the young, expectant girl going to the altar to meet her bridegroom; only to be disillusioned when the first unwanted kiss, the first wrongly-timed caress crushes her hopes; bruises them as the petals of those roses will be bruised within a few hours after she leaves me.

CHAPTER FOUR

She knew that David would not be there – would not have come back. Yet as soon as she returned to London she had to take a taxi and go to the studio to make sure. She left her luggage at the Air Terminal. The compulsion to see David was so strong that she felt quite absurdly disappointed when nobody answered her repeated knocking.

Outside in the Mews the taxi-driver was waiting. She stood there feeling deflated, disappointed, uncertain as to where to go next.

Then suddenly she thought of Patrick. She turned to the driver:

'Peacehaven Home for Crippled Ex-servicemen, Putney Hill, please!'

She stopped the taxi again as they passed a florist and bought a huge bunch of spring flowers. As they drove across the Thames she buried her face against the fragrant blooms. She remembered vividly her first meeting with Patrick.

Susan Sprees, who ran a Gossip Column in one of the papers Miranda worked for, had been giving a party. Peter, her husband, was an architect. They had a penthouse on the Embankment with a fascinating view of the Thames. Miranda was late. The party was already in full swing when she arrived. Sue saw her and immediately pushed forward a huge broad-shouldered young man whom she called 'Pat'.

'Ah! Here's the girl we've been waiting for and who I told you you'd got to meet, Pat...'

Miranda barely smiled. She was in no party mood. She had had a gruelling week; her eyes were tired; she had been to too many drink parties lately. She wanted sleep. But in the life she led, one had to keep in the swim. She often told herself that she was like a goldfish swimming madly round a bowl, only coming to the surface when she wanted food.

She glanced up at Patrick O'Mallion. He was a giant and made her feel puny. Her head just reached the tip of his chin. He had a glass of champagne in one hand and was looking down at her with eyes that were incredibly attractive, blazing beneath black lashes, and thick whimsical brows. He had a wide, smiling mouth; as typical an Irishman as she had ever seen.

'So you're Mandy!' he exclaimed.

'That's me.'

'I'm from Down Under.'

'I would have sworn you were Irish – and with that name, too.'

'Of Irish descent and never quite lost me brogue,' he said, grinning; his teeth were very white in a face that had been darkly tanned by fierce Australian suns.

'You're putting on the accent,' she chaffed.

He grinned again.

'Always heard the Irish brogue fascinated women. I'm all out to fascinate you. Sue and Peter singled you out for me this evening, otherwise I wouldn't have come.'

He looked down at her admiringly.

'You're quite a girl. Drink this...' and he pressed the champagne-cocktail into her hand.

Afterwards he told her that it was then he fell headlong in love with her. She was so slim and cool and exquisite and so elegant, too, among a lot of over-dressed and over-made-up women. She was wearing a white, pencil thin dress with a low, softly draped back. There were twisted gilt studs in her ears, and a thin gold chain encircled her throat.

Later he was to say to her:

'I had a mad desire to seize you there and then – take you into the next room where we could be alone, shut away the smoke and the sound of the screaming voices and the laughter, and then make love to you. I wanted to take off that lovely delicate dress of yours ... so that you stopped being quite so elegant and became a primitive woman.'

Yes, he had been primitive man, for sure, her crazy Patrick! Her first impression had been that he was too over-powering; but after they had talked together for a while, there seemed nobody else for her in the room – or in London.

'What are you doing tonight?' he had asked.

'Nothing,' she had lied, knowing that she was supposed to be having supper with a cousin. Inevitably she had telephoned the poor cousin to say that she was caught up by business and had to cancel her appointment. Patrick was the business. He hadn't been in London very long and didn't know it very well. He told her to choose the restaurant. She took him to a club she belonged to – underground, discreet, just off Bond Street, where the food was excellent and a Jamaican pianist played dreamy, rather sensuous music. They had danced together till long past midnight. By that time Patrick was openly declaring that he was in love with her. She no longer seemed to belong to herself. Patrick was not a person with whom you could use cold reasoning or ordinary logic. One wouldn't dream of using such words to him as *'One doesn't do this'* or *'Let me think this over'.* He gave her no time to think anything over. He had all the charm in the world with those beguiling eyes of his and that rich, drawling voice. They were weapons which he used to vanquish her long before she could put up even the most feeble fight.

But it wasn't only a question of looks with Pat. He was witty. He was, in fact, funny.

They joked and laughed together all the time. He wasn't a very good dancer – just a bit clumsy, being so huge, but their steps seemed to fit in and they danced cheek to cheek all through those long, lovely hours. They then walked along the Embankment and watched the lights on the river-craft, and turned now and again to kiss each other with an abandonment that was as fierce as it was sudden.

'You use shock tactics,' she had told him, shakily.

'One has to, with a girl like you. I daren't give you time to be sensible. I know how intelligent you are. I want you idiotic – about me, mavourneen.'

'Oh, Patrick!' she had laughed and shaken her head.

She was to make that exclamation many times during the weeks that followed. But when she was with him the next day she refused to kiss him. She was herself again – a more cautious, aloof Miranda. She wasn't going to be 'bulldozed' – she told him so. He grinned and shrugged his wide shoulders.

'Okay – shure and I'll wait till you shed that civilized veneer again, me lovely darlin'!'

Patrick's boisterous spirits and hot vigorous youth had a stunning effect on her. He was so absolutely male; physically he towered above most of his friends and was several inches broader. It was impossible to overlook him in a crowd and she soon found that it was impossible to ignore him. He bombarded her with invitations to parties, to the races, to football and ice-hockey matches, car rallies, week-end house-parties with his hospitable friends who seemed to be as uninhibited as himself. He literally swept her off her feet, carrying her along with him in a wild rush of physical activity which although she found it exhausting, gradually became a stimulant – a necessity in her life.

Unlike Ludwig with his quiet, deep intellect, Patrick was a Philistine who lived through the enjoyment of the senses. His love of people, of crowds, of big noisy gatherings, was infectious – like his incessant laughter. He made friends wherever he went. He could not stay still. Even in a cinema he would fidget and seldom managed to sit through to the end of a film.

After two months Miranda called a halt.

'I just can't go out tonight!' she told him firmly. 'I want to do some ironing. I have three articles to turn in to the office tomorrow morning and I must, must, MUST have some sleep!'

At once he was all apologies. He had fatigued her unmercifully. He had been inconsiderate, thoughtless. Well, now he would be different. His darling Mandy, his mavourneen would see that he *could* be different, could simmer down and stay 'put'.

'Wait here!' he said, as if he thought she might have intended to run out of her flat away from him like an Irish sprite.

Within the hour, he was back with a hamper of food and telling her gaily that they would share a quiet evening together.

'No cooking – it's all here. No washing up – we'll eat cold duck with our fingers; no coffee to make, I've got champagne. And afterwards I'll sit and read the evening paper while you write your articles.'

Of course, it hadn't worked out that way. They had barely started on the food before Patrick realized he had bought sufficient for six people.

'Darlin', shure an' we can't waste it' he said in his rich brogue. 'Let's ask Peter and Sue to share it. They only live a stone's-throw from here and I know you'd like them. I'll tell them they've got to vamoose the moment the meal's over.'

Peter and Susan were glad to come. They were in good spirits. The champagne exhilarated Miranda, and Patrick was, as usual, captivating. Within the space of a few hours another party was in full swing and Miranda never did do any work.

In quiet moments at the office – the only quiet moments she knew now! – Miranda tried to think about this strange friendship. For so it was. Patrick monopolized her time, sent her flowers, lived on the telephone to her when he was not actually with her and paid her compliments by the thousands. She was his 'darling mavourneen!' She was stunning; all the stars in the firmament. She amused him, too; she was more fun than any girl he'd met in Australia; she was the best dancer... He seemed to grow genuinely fond of her and he showed it in a hundred little ways. But came the day in Miranda's flat when he told her that tomorrow he was leaving for Australia.

It was a warm June afternoon. The hum and boom of London traffic drifted through the open windows, breaking into the silence that followed the announcements of his departure.

Miranda had washed her hair. She was drying it in the late sunshine when he burst in upon her. He stood now, seeming to crowd the room with his large frame. He was silent for once, his eyes serious and reflective as he watched her. She looked young – younger than she really was with that damp hair rough-curling against her white neck. A woman washing or drying her hair was a charming sight – a favourite study for an artist. Patrick was no artist but he could not help admiring Miranda – even more than usual.

'I'm sorry, Patrick!' she said, truthfully. 'Truly sorry. It's been such fun.'

More than that, she thought. It's been just

what I needed so badly when I ran away from Ludwig. If I'd been too much alone, had too much time to think and remember, I might have weakened and gone back to Paris. I know now that it wasn't the life I needed. I wanted to be young, irresponsible – to have fun!

He came and stood behind her, his large hands strangely gentle as they caressed her damp, soft hair.

'Come with me, mavourneen!'

She looked up at him uncertainly, trying to read his face which was usually so amiable and happy but in this hour had a look of strain, even of misery.

'I love you. I've known hundreds of girls but never one I wanted to marry. Come to Australia, to my home and marry me, Mandy.'

She stood silent, feeling awkward, and deeply moved. The towel slid from her fingers and she rubbed them together with a slow, nervous gesture. He seized those hands suddenly; then pulled her close and kissed her.

It was a lover's kiss, deep, exploring, hurting her soft mouth. Then as suddenly he let her go. His breathing was rapid – his face flushed and his eyes warm and triumphant in a proud, male way.

'So you do love me, darling,' he said, delightedly. 'I didn't just imagine it. You feel for me as I do for you. There's magic on your lips, mavourneen. Come and sit down with me while I tell you about Australia.'

She did not refuse but went slowly with him. Her body was betraying her again, she thought cynically. She wanted to be loved and taken by this crazy, marvellous Irishman.

They sat close together on the sofa. He kept an arm around her as he started to talk.

'It's a beautiful country, big and grand and clean,' he told her. 'I'll take you in a ship along the Great Barrier Reef. There you'll find true magic in the colour of the sea. It sparkles – it's a transparent green where it covers the coral reef, and deepens to darkest blue where the reefs are carved away to deep pools and chasms. I'll take you in a glass-bottomed dory where you can lie and look below the rippled surface and watch the tiny coloured fish darting under the water. The world of coral is like a fabulous painting in the Arabian Nights, a galaxy of jewels – rose-pink, aquamarine, sapphire, brilliant red, green, and violet. The coral grows like a tree in an exotic flower garden; sometimes it piles into lofty peaks and crags and rises like the towers and spirals of some chimerical castle.'

She listened, entranced.

He took her with him into the dazzling dream of his coral reef. She closed her eyes and tried to imagine this new world he was picturing for her.

'The fishes have glorious colours. They dart in and out of the natural caves; you'll see them – coral cod, bronze-coloured with fluorescent spots of turquoise blue; parrot fish like bright tropical parakeets; yellow-tails that have mother-of-pearl sides and bright golden tails; zebra fish striped with black and silver. We'll spend our honeymoon there, Mandy. You'll think it the most beautiful place in the whole world. You can collect shells on the beach and pick coral sprigs and I'll make you necklaces and turn you into a mermaid. I'll take you to see the volcanic islands, wooded and desolate. We'll lie together on beaches of silver sand. We'll bathe and pick coconuts and drink the warm, sweet milk. I'll cover you with wild white orchids. There'll be only the two of us and perhaps a flock of white, yellow-crested cockatoos to call us – laugh with us.'

She went on listening, astonished by the imagination in his words – the unexpected artistry of Patrick's symphonic poem.

He laughed suddenly now and squeezed Miranda's arm.

'Oh, mavourneen – it's grand. Then I'll take you to my home in Queensland. We have a big sheep-station there. You'll like it. The sun shines almost without ceasing. The climate is tropical. You'll have your own horse and we'll ride together; I'll take you fishing in the river. We'll cook the small blue fish we catch, on a fire – out of doors. Evenings, we'll give parties, and dance in the big old barn. We'll be among friends – good friends – ready to laugh and love as we do. Oh, Mandy, will you come?'

He fell silent then, waiting for her to speak; to pronounce judgement on the glittering world he had created for her.

She said at last:

'It was glorious – just listening to you. I can imagine it all so vividly. It sounds like paradise. I know it could be – but I don't know if I could marry you, Patrick. I don't know if I love you enough, you see. I think it would be very easy to fall in love with you but I can't be sure – not yet. I need time to think it over.'

He gave a quick, pleased laugh.

'Okay, I'll not be rushing you, if that's all it is, mavourneen. Maybe it's best that I don't take you with me tomorrow for I'll only be home a couple of weeks before I do a spell in Korea.'

'Korea?'

'Sure. I offered my services before I came to England on holiday. I doubt it will be for long. They say it'll all be over in a few months – perhaps before I even get out there.'

'But why do *you* have to go?'

He leaned forward, clasping his big hands together.

'Because I want to! I wasn't old enough to see action in the last war and I thought I'd like to put in a spoke for freedom somehow before I settle down to raising sheep for the rest of my life.'

She nodded. She liked that streak in him. It was half his charm. But to be killed or mutilated in the Korean war – no, that made her shudder. He wouldn't be cautious, this one. He would have no regard for his life. He would fight as he would love – hotly and recklessly.

'I'll like being out there all the better, knowing you're waiting for me,' he added. 'When I'm free, I'll come back for you. Now kiss me, me darlin', for time is getting short.'

She wanted to speak – to discuss it all; to analyse and probe in her feminine fashion. But he wanted her and he pulled her across his lap and his mouth came down on hers.

Patrick's kisses were as wild and exciting as his way of life. She forgot Ludwig, forgot her own earlier vows never to let a man make love to her unless she knew she truly loved him. Patrick gave her no time to make up her mind. He possessed her with a kind of ruthless passion and her own young body responded to the primitive, uncalculated desires of his. Their union in this hour was as it had once been with David – an unbridled giving and taking that knew no restraint. Her clothes were there on the carpet – a silken heap. Her white, beautiful body was all his and his hard fierce masculinity belonged to her.

'Has it ever been like this for you before?' he asked her, his lips against her breast.

'No,' she lied to please him. 'It never has.'

'Do I please you?'

She stroked his brown, square face. The curls were damp, like a boy's, she thought, across his forehead.

'Yes – yes – you do.'

She had never known a man so ardent. He had fanned her own desires into a kind of madness. With Patrick that night, love was a wonderful, devastating battle which they fought in order to reach the quintessence – the ultimate of pleasure, and their surrender was mutual.

She seemed to ache with love. She accepted Patrick in the spirit in which he gave himself. It was, she supposed, pure, unadulterated passion, quite unlike anything else she had experienced in her life before. But not without friendliness and tenderness. Man though he was, Patrick still continued to seem like a big delightful boy whom she wanted to please. It was not as it had been with the others, when all she wanted was to be cradled, petted and pleased. All that Patrick gave her she wanted to give back – and did.

'You're the most exciting woman I've ever held in my arms,' he told her. 'There could never be another like you, marvourneen. You're in my blood now and I don't want to get you out. I only want to be allowed to go on loving you for ever.'

When the loving and the caressing were over, he kissed her tenderly. In the quiet hours that followed as they lay side by side in the darkness, talking, she came to know him a little better; to love him a little more; to gain some insight into the life she might lead with him.

If indeed, she decided to follow him at a later date to Australia, she knew that she would miss the intellectual stimulus of a less physically-minded man. Patrick's was a simple world in which he enjoyed a purely sensuous existence. His happiness came from a perfectly-made healthy body, from the sunshine, from swimming and riding, from life out of doors. His mind was completely satisfied by the friendship and company of other people and Miranda knew that her life would be rich in this way if she married him. It would be rich materially, too, for the family farm covered a huge area of ground. His income would allow him to give her all that the average woman would want in her home, or outside it. Holidays, cars, horses, parties, and children – a big family if they wanted one.

Perhaps, she thought, she would not have time to miss the operas, the art exhibitions, the good plays and films out there in Australia. Life would be untrammelled and in many ways nearer to the kind the Almighty must have intended when he made the world; before people herded into cities, formed societies, and restricted their own freedom.

'You'll marry me, won't you, Mandy?' he asked her once more when they made love again in the cool, quiet, shadowy hours of dawn. 'I wish now I hadn't enlisted for Korea. How could I know I was going to meet you!'

She wound her arms tightly round his shoulders, feeling with her fingertips the taut strength of his muscular back. With the aftermath of lovemaking, she felt close to him in spirit as well as in body. Real happiness for both of them seemed possible. Absolute love? Perhaps not! But in its place passion, fondness, warm friendship which could precede the birth of love.

Looking back now, Miranda knew that she had never loved Patrick. She had been in love with him that one night. She had lain in his arms, and but for the cruel fate which had overtaken him, it might have become something more. As it was, Patrick went back to Australia and for the best part of a year she had only his letters to make his brief visit to England seem a reality. She still had those letters. Once in a while she had retrieved them from the attic – during evenings when John had been away. She had read them wonderingly:

'*My sweet love,*

Home somehow seems to have lost its beauty and true meaning as you are not here to share in it with me. However, the family have given me a fine welcome and are crazy about your picture. They can't wait to meet you and Dad is writing to tell you to come along and visit them any time you can – even if I'm in Korea.

My darling, we didn't discuss dull things like money but I guess you may not have the air fare over so I'm wiring the money to your bank. You're to draw on it for anything you want. If you feel like visiting Australia to give it the once-over, I'd love to know you were there, but if you're happier in your own flat, amongst your friends, I don't want you to feel you must come – at least, not until I get back from Korea.

I keep thinking about your glorious body and can't wait to hold you in my arms again. We had some fine moments, mavourneen, didn't we? At night, I can't sleep for thinking of you, so pale and sad and golden, and yet you could laugh, too. Strange, Miranda. There's no one like you in the world.'

Another letter from Korea in answer to a long one from her:

91

'Do you think the past matters to me, mavourneen? That you'd been divorced I knew already from one of our mutual friends. About the fellow in Paris – I guess that was part of growing-up. I'm no saint, Mandy, and there have been many women in my life – too many – but you know, I never felt the desire to be faithful till I met you. The past doesn't matter – the future is everything and I'm waiting impatiently for your decision. I know I promised to give you time to think it over, but I'm so sure I could be happy with you, I can't bring myself to believe you wouldn't be happy, too. Yet even as I write this, I realize it doesn't always work out that way. However, if you can write at least that you do love me a little, it'll cheer me up a lot in this pretty horrible place. We're moving around a lot, so I hope this reaches you okay. I thank my lucky stars I took my pilot's training after the war. I think I told you we have a small private plane at home for spotting sheep and getting around more quickly. I'd sure hate to be on the ground in this war. I'm seeing plenty of action and find it exciting if tiring.'

In his next letter he had enclosed a snapshot of himself in flying kit, looking tanned and incredibly handsome – a tall, dark, young god of the skies.

'It's getting pretty hot and I don't just mean the

weather. I'm beginning to feel there never existed another life and I cling to your memory and thoughts of home. I don't think you realize, mavourneen, how much I love you – quite what the thought of you in this wild place means to me. Your picture is like an oasis in a desert of killing and destruction. War is terrible. Maybe when I get home, I'll give more time to planning World Peace – there must be some way we could help – something we could do. If nothing else, we might open a home to some of these pathetic refugees.

'*Oh, Mandy, my love – you haunt my dream and I long for your cool sweet body and the touch of your hands. I never longed for anything so much in my life before.*'

She sensed a new, more serious side to him. After his experiences in Korea he would not be the same carefree, superficial, happy-go-lucky person. She welcomed this new thoughtfulness even while she worried for his safety and prayed for all the people involved in the war. This new Patrick she could love more fully – with her mind as well as her body.

She wrote trying to explain this new feeling to him.

'*I think I would like to go out to Australia and meet your family,*' she added, knowing this would bring him happiness, too.

But he did not reply and for three weeks she had no word from him. Then came his father's letter telling her Patrick had been shot down and was being flown to Japan for urgent hospital treatment. At once she cabled back, asking for further news as soon as it was available.

'If desirable, could fly to Japan,' she added to her cablegram

But even while she started the complicated routine of preparing visas, passport, tickets, leave from the office, a further letter was on its way to her.

'Patrick had multiple injuries to his face and body. His back is broken. I'm leaving today for Japan will write to you at once when I have seen him and confirmed this terrible report.'

During the days that followed, she lived in a nightmare of fear – prayed as she had never prayed before, but the next report gave no softening of the blow. Even if he lived he would never walk again.

It was almost a year before she saw him. He was flown to London for a special operation and she received a telephone call from a fellow Australian.

'He wants to talk to you, but only on certain conditions. This isn't easy to put but I'll do my best. He gave me to understand you were half-way to becoming engaged. Well, that's all off. He doesn't want pity from you and he says any question of marriage is quite out for him now. If you go, it is to be as a friend – no more.'

It had been hard not to show her pity – hard to pretend a casual friendship when she was torn with horror at the way Patrick's beautiful face and body had been mutilated. Even his spirit had been a little broken then.

But with each visit it became easier and with each passing month, Patrick's spirit healed and he ceased to wish himself dead. She took books and engendered his initiation into the escape of reading; brought him a record-player and stimulated a natural love of rhythm, a love of light opera, and forward to the classics. Love was never mentioned but in its place, friendship blossomed. It became a habit to visit him regularly. Never had she allowed more than a month or two to pass without spending a day with him.

By the time the doctors had finished with him, Patrick had made up his mind not to go back to Australia.

'Home is a place for the young and active,' he said, but calmly – without bitterness.

He was moved to the Peacehaven Home for Crippled Ex-Servicemen in Putney and taught to make baskets and mats with his hands. At Miranda's suggestion, he tried painting but gave it up in favour of a typewriter.

'Thank God, I can still use my fingers,' he said.

Only once had she tried to speak of their former relationship and had been cut short with such a violence of emotion, she never dared try again. She must respect his pride and desire for independence if she wished to keep his friendship.

How wise he had been, she told herself today as the taxi-driver drew up at the Home and she walked the familiar long corridor to Patrick's ward. Over the years they had stayed good friends. She had helped him to begin a career in journalism, writing stories with an Australian background. In time he had drawn from her the news of her activities in the outside world, and it was Patrick who had known even before John did, that she had decided to accept John's proposal of marriage.

'Good on you, Mandy!' he had replied. 'I was wondering when you would.'

He looked round as she came into the ward carrying the narcissi and freesias and smiled a welcome, shifting the typewriter on the frame above his chest so that he could hold out a hand to her.

'It's ages since I saw you, mavourneen. What's been happening to you? Mmm, lovely!' he added, sniffing the flowers.

Briefly, she told him. It was possible now to tell Patrick anything without fear of hurting him. He was fully adjusted to his limited existence.

'Hell, I'm sorry!' he said. 'Wish I could suggest a way out. Maybe you just have to find that first husband of yours in order to sort yourself out.'

She looked down into those blue handsome eyes, the only part of Patrick to remain unchanged, and thought suddenly:

If he hadn't been shot down, would I have married him? Would I have been happy in Australia? Was Patrick – the man he used to be – the one I might really have loved?

Suddenly she saw him smile.

'I know what you are thinking, mavourneen. You're wondering whether *we* would have made the grade together. And don't look so surprised – I'm not telepathic, I just know you pretty well by now!'

She smiled back at him, glad they could talk so easily of the past.

'Admit you *like* me better now than ever you did ten years ago!' he said quickly. 'You were attracted to me then but *I wasn't on your level, Mandy.* I'd never learned to use my mind, only my body. Now I've had to, and I'm probably much nearer spiritually to being the kind of guy you could live with – but you can't live with a cripple. You need the life of the body, too – both must exist in harmony for you to live at all.'

She looked at him bewildered. He was right – he knew her better than she knew herself.

'What shall I do, Patrick? I hate hurting John. My life seems to have been a useless search for something that is quite intangible. Maybe I should stop wanting the impossible for myself and start trying to give.'

'Perhaps it is only when you have found what you are seeking that you will be able to give in the way you mean.'

They talked of other things, too – Patrick's work – his parents who were coming over to England to visit him in the summer.

'They still hope I'll go home,' he said half-ruefully. 'Maybe I will – for a long holiday. Dad says they can fly me home on a stretcher, and the same round our estate. But I couldn't live there now. After so long in this old place, it feels like home to me.'

Tears, sudden and unbidden, stung her eyes.

'Don't weep for me, mavourneen,' Patrick said softly, holding her hand. 'I am content. I have my work, my friends, and one of the most beautiful women in the world to count among them. I have much in my life that is worthwhile and I would never now end it the way I once thought of doing.'

'You have courage, my dear, *very* dear Patrick,' she said, wiping her eyes. 'Lend me a little of it, I need it more than you do!'

CHAPTER FIVE

The visit to Patrick made its impression on her. Miranda returned to Victoria to retrieve her luggage. In the station she sat down to think and drank a cup of tea served by an elderly, tired waitress. As she sat there, staring at the constantly changing crowd of people, she felt insignificant, lonely and somehow a little cheap.

If Patrick could learn to accept life – even to enjoy it – despite his terrible handicap, what right had she to complain because some nebulous satisfaction seemed to be missing in her own pampered existence? She had so much, as John's wife. She watched in particular the thin, weary waitress, whose hair was all tight curls and whose hollow cheeks were rouged, like her lips, in a pathetic attempt to be attractive. She felt ashamed of herself. If *this* was her life – a struggle to earn a living for herself and perhaps a family – or to eke out a dull existence on an old-age pension, then she might have been justified in complaining; believing with resentment that there must be something more satisfying elsewhere.

When she asked for her bill, she spoke to

the woman.

'Tell me, are *you* happy?'

A look of surprise crossed the waitress's face.

'That's a queer question, luv! I suppose I am – don't know as I ever think about that sort of thing much – don't have time. Are you a reporter?'

'I was once. Not now.'

The waitress's gaze travelled with curiosity and admiration over the beautiful, well-dressed figure.

'Once a reporter, always a reporter, I dare say,' she sniffed. 'Well, since you ask, I make out quite nicely, thank you. My old man has been good to me – he never was a big earner but he wasn't like some I could mention, drinking away their wages something disgraceful. My kids is all grown up and married and I see my grandchildren once a week – I look forward to that. Then there's Saturday nights – we always go out on Saturdays to the "Pig and Whistle". Rare old sing-song we have, too?'

'And your work? Don't you get very tired?'

'Wore out, luv. But you see a bit of life in this job – all sorts you get in a place like a big station. And the money's quite good. We're saving for a telly. Want the cash before we buy. Me and my old man don't believe in 'ire purchase.'

On an impulse, Miranda slipped a ten-shilling note into the waitress's hand and cut short the profusion of thanks. The woman looked as though she was going to burst into tears.

She sat on after the waitress had gone, smoking and thinking. As John's wife she had so much more than millions of other women – why then leave what she had to follow a hopeless trail which would only end in further disillusionment?

David – the name hung persistently on the fringe of her thoughts. But even if she contacted him – with what purpose? Did she anticipate finding that she was still in love with him? Or that she might fall in love with him all over again? Supposing David had no interest in her and had found someone else? Even if they both regretted their broken marriage, would either trust a repetition of it? And would it – any of it – be fair to poor John?

She lit a cigarette and smoked reflectively. She knew that she owed John too much for her peace of mind. There had been years of material comforts, of incessant acts of kindness and attention. In his own way, he loved her. He hadn't failed. *She had.*

She thought of the last few days – Alastair, Ludwig, Patrick – all of them men she might have married. She reached the definite conclusion that in no case would it have worked. If Alastair hadn't taken to drink; if

Ludwig had been younger; if Patrick hadn't been crippled; oh, yes, there was always an IF.

She passed her hand nervously across her forehead. There was still Tony and *David* – but might she not eventually arrive at the same deadlock – the same IF, blocking the way to happiness?

Suddenly, she knew she must go home to John. She would go now, at once, and for the first time in her life make a really conscious effort to be the sort of wife he wanted, and so find her own happiness and salvation.

She got up, hurried out to the taxi-rank and took a cab to Eaton Place – to her home.

Mrs Woods opened the door and for once her good training was swept aside on the wave of surprise.

'Good gracious, Madam, I wasn't expecting you!'

'I know, Mrs Woods. I didn't have time to let you know.'

'Is Mr Villiers home?'

'He should be in later, Madam. He ordered dinner for half past eight. I'll call Nina to make your bed and switch on the central heating. We turned out the bedroom after you went away. I took the liberty of sending your eiderdown to the cleaners. You remember, there was a coffee stain on it.'

Miranda gave the woman a charming, friendly smile which endeared her to her staff. It was a smile that eliminated 'class differences and reassured those whose wages she paid that she cared about them.' The pleasure in Mrs Woods' eyes on seeing her again touched and comforted Miranda. It was a welcome. And as Mrs Woods took her fur coat from her and hurried away, she realized how much she had missed the little personal attentions she had received here, although she had not been aware of it while she was away. No luxury hotel in the world could provide the feeling of warmth and intimacy that she experienced in her own home.

She walked through the hall slowly, looking around the familiar surroundings. It was a charming Regency house. When she and John had first bought it, John had spent a lot of money on the interior decoration to suit her taste which he shared. Together they had decided on the enlargement of the entrance hall which now incorporated many of the small back rooms and cupboards.

The paint was white – pure white. Through an archway at one end of the house Miranda could see the beautiful Italian marble table on gilt carved legs. She loved that table. On it she always kept two ormolu candlesticks and a huge bowl of flowers. The bowl tonight was full of spring flowers, rather like the ones she had taken to poor Patrick. Above the table hung a new Graham Sutherland – it was John who liked Sutherland and was proud to own this painting.

The sight of so much beauty and the expensive taste that John had indulged brought her a fresh feeling of guilt.

The staircase was splendid – the carved rosewood banister was unique. The carpets throughout were a dark, glorious green. Through the open door on the right she could see into her drawing-room; the shell-backed open cupboard in the wall – its shelves full of exquisite china; the white carpet; the scarlet satin studded sofa and chairs; the deep turquoise of the French silk paper which they had chosen and brought especially from Paris. She remembered what a thrill it had been to find curtains of the same glorious turquoise, threaded with a design of silver leaves. She moved forward impulsively and switched on the light because she loved to see that soft golden glow from the two alabaster lamps on either side of the Adam fireplace. She watched the scintillating reflection of the lights on the chased shining surface of the Venetian mirror which they had brought back from Italy, and felt renewed pride and pleasure in the beauty of her home.

Then she switched out the lights again and turned back into the hall. She felt suddenly tired and uncomfortable. She knew that she must look ungroomed. She wanted a bath – she wanted to change everything that she had on and to make herself look really fresh and lovely before John came home.

Later, while she lay soaking in hot perfumed water in her bathroom, Nina chatted to her from the bedroom.

'It is so splendid to have the *Señora* home. The house is sad without the *Señora*. What will you wear this evening?'

'Oh, I don't think I'll put on a long evening dress,' Miranda called back, amused and touched by Nina's obvious admiration and interest in her.

'Albert say the *Señor* was wearing a dinner-jacket, *Señora.*'

Miranda came through into her bedroom swathed in a blue bath robe. With a small towel she rubbed the back of her neck. She felt gloriously refreshed.

'The *Señor* has changed already? Has he been home, then?'

'*Si, Señora.* He was home about half past five and he change to go out again at seven o'clock. He say dinner to be at half past eight.'

A little puzzled, Miranda started to put on the gossamer pale-blue lingerie Nina had laid on her bed.

Perhaps John had gone to his Club for a drink? It seemed strange he should be wearing a dinner-jacket.

'All right, Nina – I'll wear the white.'

Nina slipped the beautifully-cut, creamy-white sheath dress over her employer's head and zipped up the back. The dress clung to Miranda's hips and breasts and left her smooth rounded shoulders bare. It was the most expensive dress she had ever bought – a Balmain – and John had greatly admired it. Several of her women friends whose opinions she valued even more than John's used to be ecstatic about the model. It was in fact very becoming; it accentuated her flawless figure and its very simplicity flattered her beauty.

Nina brushed her mistress's thick fair hair across the back of her head and wound the ends into a Spanish comb.

'Ze emeralds, *Señora?*' Nina worshipped jewellery.

Miranda drew a line of blue on both eyelids then shook her head, smiling.

'Last time I wore this dress, you tried to make me wear emeralds. I don't want anything with it, Nina, except my gold bracelets.'

The girl sighed. It seemed a waste to have such a magnificent collection of jewels, real ones, too, and then not wear any of them. Still, the *Señora* looked perfect. Nina wished her Spanish cousin, Adimenita who worked in Selfridges, could see her. Like a film star the *Señora* was, when she dressed like this!

Feeling slightly more self-assured, Miranda went downstairs to the drawing-room. She glanced at the tiny gold and enamel clock on the bookcase and saw that it was just after eight. John would surely be back soon.

She felt a wave of unaccustomed nervousness. How was she going to explain to him her sudden unaccountable decision to come home? Who would speak the first words?

'John, I hope you don't mind...'

No, that was silly.

'Hullo, John ... I've decided to come back...'

Too abrupt.

Say nothing, she told herself uneasily. Let him do the talking.

'Well, this is a pleasant surprise...'

She jumped as the sound of voices came from the hall. She hadn't heard his key in the front door. She turned her head and the drawing-room door opened and John came in. He wasn't alone. There was another man with him – a man whose face seemed vaguely familiar but whose name she had forgotten. And there were two women – young, smart and beautifully dressed – both strangers to Miranda.

She rose at once and stood uncertainly, her back to the fireplace. For a brief instant, she thought she saw a frown follow the look of astonishment in John's eyes. Then he came forward and gave her a quick kiss on one cheek.

'I'm so glad you managed to get back in time after all, Mandy. I was pretty sure you wouldn't make it so this is a nice surprise. Now, let me introduce you to my guests. Mrs Ingleby, my wife; John Ingleby, I think you have met before, haven't you, at the Hunt Ball. And Mrs Van de Haal, my wife!'

Miranda had a swift impression of a cool, appraising stare from the last of John's guests. Then in a slow American drawl, Mrs Van de Haal said:

'How nice to meet you, Mrs Villiers. John has told me *SO* much about you.'

John was busy now dispensing drinks from the corner cupboard. Miranda could expect no help from him. She felt a strange hostility, although for the moment she could think of no reason why this stranger should dislike her. Like most American society women, she was perfectly groomed – and very *chic,* if a little over-dressed. With a smile, Miranda thought that Nina would have approved of that magnificent diamond brooch and bracelets. Against the black velvet dinner gown they were stunning – and real! Whoever this woman was, she was certainly rich. She said:

'John told me you were abroad, Mrs Villiers. Paris, I believe. Did you go to see the Collections, or were you too late? I adore Paris in the Spring.'

The American rattled on. Miranda made a non-commital reply. She found herself wondering how John had known she was in Paris. She hadn't written ... at least not to him. Nina might have shown him the post-card. She forgot the problem as John handed her a sherry.

Only then did she realize that coming home unexpectedly, she had inadvertently disorganised John's dinner party. Now there were too many women – and she was the odd one out. Perhaps she should make an apology, say she was going out – but after John's greeting that might seem peculiar. Obviously, he meant her to pretend that he'd *known* she might turn up.

She excused herself as soon as it was possible to do so and went quickly into the dining-room. Mrs Woods was lighting the candles.

'I've laid the extra place for you, Madam, here between Mr and Mrs Ingleby. I've put the American lady on Mr Villiers's right.'

Miranda nodded. She felt suddenly terribly tired and wondered how she would manage to get through this brittle, social evening. It was a pity Mrs Woods hadn't warned her – but she must have presumed Miranda had been in touch with her husband!

It was an excellent dinner. Fortunately, Miranda found both Mr Ingleby and his wife charming and easy to talk to. Mrs Van de

Haal chatted ceaselessly in her high, droning voice to John who did not seem to be irritated by the shrillness of it, as Miranda was. She gathered from the Inglebys that Mrs Van de Haal was their guest, on a prolonged visit to England. Recently she had lost her husband – a baked-bean manufacturer of Dutch descent. He had left his widow a substantial fortune.

'I used to know Cassie when she and I were at finishing school in Paris,' Mrs Ingleby told Miranda. 'We kept in touch and I was her guest in North Carolina for six months before I married. This is the first chance I've had to return the hospitality – after all these years, too. I suddenly had a letter from Cassie telling me that her husband had died and that she wanted to get away for a while, so of course we invited her to stay with us.'

The Merry Widow! Miranda thought wryly. Maybe John had seemed a likely substitute for the baked-bean magnate!

While the men stayed on at the table for cigars and brandy, Miranda took the two women up to her bedroom. Mrs Van de Haal did not trouble to conceal her interest in the room. Miranda felt sure that she was checking up on the number of pillows on the double bed and searching for a glimpse of any article belonging to John which might suggest he shared the room with her.

'My husband's room is through there!' she said at last, pointing to an adjoining door. 'As I'm a very light sleeper, I just can't have him in with me. He snores so badly.'

She felt like a schoolgirl as she told this lie but didn't regret it when she saw the puzzled expression on the American woman's face. It was an attractive face in its way, high cheekbones, black smooth hair, almond-shaped eyes accentuated by blue shadows; beautiful but spoiled by the thinness of the lips, a woman of experience, of style. She wondered now if John had told the Van de Haals that they were temporarily separated and that this woman was aware of the fact.

The men were not long in joining them downstairs for coffee. At once, Mrs Van de Haal broke off her discussion with Mrs Ingleby and turned her attention to John, patting the place beside her on the sofa.

'Say, John – how goes it? Come and talk to me.'

Miranda wasn't so much jealous as amused. Her earlier feeling of being *de trop* vanished as she realized that the American woman was not very subtle. It couldn't be long before John must see through the surface to her barely-concealed efforts to attract. He had always liked women to be a little remote, even Victorian, in their reserve and old-fashioned femininity. Cassandra wasn't his type.

He was very attentive to her, but Miranda soon began to wonder, uneasily, whether her being here was spoiling his fun. After each little courtesy he paid his guests, his eyes would turn swiftly to his wife and away again as though he were embarrassed.

Mrs Van de Haal suggested a game of bridge but nobody else appeared much in favour of this as there were five of them. John offered to play some new records but no-one seemed much inclined to listen to music. They preferred to talk. Miranda became more and more silent – depressed. The evening flagged and ended early. The Ingleby's removed a reluctant Mrs Van de Haal soon after half past eleven. As the front door closed behind them, Miranda drew a breath of relief.

She was amazed when John turned on her while they were still in the hall, and said in a low, angry tone:

'Another time you decide to use our house as a hotel, you might have the courtesy to let me know beforehand that you're arriving. I've never been so embarrassed in my life.'

She stood still, her pale skin reddening, her pulse giving a fitful, unpleasant jerk. For a second she stared. She said, coldly:

'I'm very sorry. I'd no idea you were bringing guests to dinner. Mrs Woods never told me – I suppose she took it for granted I knew.'

John followed her into the drawing-room and poured himself a whisky and soda. Miranda stood with her back to the fireplace. She waited for him to speak. She felt absolutely flattened and not a little perturbed.

'How long are you staying?' he demanded.

She bit her lip. Of the many things he might have said, she didn't expect this question.

'I don't know!' she replied. 'I – I just made up my mind suddenly this afternoon to come home.'

'Was it Paris or the *paramour* that didn't come up to expectations?'

Burning colour now swept across Miranda's face. She sat down, too surprised, too angry to make an immediate reply. John must have been having her followed. How else could he have known she had visited Ludwig? She flung back her head – her face changing now from red to white. She was shaking.

'When I left home, it was *not* with the idea of rushing into someone else's arms, John. I thought you knew me well enough to be certain at least that I'd always be honest with you. If there had been a – a lover, I'd have told you.'

His back was still towards her but he swung round now and faced her. His eyes were angry and bitter.

'You don't deny you went to see your

painter friend?'

'Of course I don't deny it. Before that, I went to see another man, someone you don't know. Today, I saw Patrick whom you have met. I suppose you've been having me followed, John. Well, don't waste your money, please. If you want a report of my movements, I will supply you with it myself.'

He turned away from her. The apology he wanted to make remained stuck in his throat.

'You don't seem exactly to have been wasting your time, either!' Miranda added furiously. 'I can't say I particularly admire your taste in women, John. Unless, of course, you are dazzled by Mrs Van de Haal's diamonds, which doesn't seem very likely.'

'Will you be quiet!' His voice cut her short. 'Mrs Van de Haal is a very well-informed and charming woman.'

As suddenly as it had come, Miranda felt her anger vanish and in its place crept a cold, quiet dismay. This angry, absurd quarrel was the last thing in the world she had come home for. She had wanted – oh, she wasn't altogether certain quite what she had wanted – but not this, *not this*.

Near to tears, she stood up.

'I'm going up to bed. I'm sorry about tonight. If I do come back again, I'll let you know first.'

He looked at her sullenly. Then his hand

came out as though to restrain her, but he let it fall back. She was too hurt to lower her pride and stay of her own accord. If John wanted her to stay at home, he must say so. It was up to him now to make the next move.

In the privacy of her bedroom, Miranda flung herself down on her bed and laid her hot cheeks against the cool linen of the small frilled pillow she always used. She no longer wanted to cry. But she felt deeply hurt – hurt in a way a child might be if it had held out both arms and been rejected.

She tried to think coolly, to reason with her head and not with her heart. If John had had her followed, it could mean one of two things – either that he wanted evidence so he could divorce her; or that he merely wanted to know one way or another if she was being unfaithful to him. If the latter were true, then it could only mean that he still loved her and was jealous. Was this so? Had his slightly-exaggerated attention to Mrs Van de Haal tonight been because he had entertained a spiteful wish to make Miranda jealous? She wasn't jealous. She had no right to be. But she didn't like the idea of John in the power of such a stupid, conceited woman like Cassie Van de Haal. What a *name*, Miranda kept thinking, with a touch of hysteria in the humour.

He had seemed genuinely angry that she had spoiled his dinner party. Certainly she had made him look a bit foolish in front of his guests. He must have told them his wife was away. But could loss of pride really be of more importance than her return to him?

She stared thoughtfully at the golden light of her bedside lamp. Did she care? Would she really mind, deep deep down inside, if John had stopped loving her? Was it only her own pride that would be hurt – not her deepest self?

All her nerves tightened suddenly as she heard John's bedroom door open. A moment later, she heard him moving around. Was he coming in here? She drew in her breath and waited.

There came a knock on the door and she swung into a sitting position, her heart thudding violently.

'Come in!'

John walked into the room. He carried a tray of tea.

'Mrs Woods brought this into the drawing-room just after you left. She said she felt sure you'd want one, as you usually do.'

That touched her, but she spoke coolly.

'Oh, thank you.'

She took the tray from him and put it on her bedside table. Not so long ago she and John used to drink tea together like this in here after dinner-parties, discussing their guests in warm, after-party friendliness. Tonight he seemed a stranger. He looked implacable, she thought, absolutely without tenderness for her.

'Do you want a cup?'

'Er, no, no thank you. I've just had a whisky. Well, if there's nothing else you want, I suppose I'd better turn in. I've quite a day at the office tomorrow.'

John! *John!*

But the name was only in her mind. She could not voice it. It seemed as if he were deaf to her unspoken cry. If he would only stay, sweep her into his arms and kiss and caress her; stimulate her to a physical longing so that they could be reunited at least to some degree by their physical intimacy! But that was not John's way with a woman. He had always held back – waited for her to indicate that she wished him to sleep with her. He wasn't exactly hesitant as a lover but almost from the beginning he had expected her to make the first move.

Why couldn't he see that this was an occasion when she needed him to take the initiative and show a fierce, demanding passion? Without it, her own emotions would remain quiescent.

'Sure there's nothing else you want?' he asked.

'Yes! No – I mean, I don't want anything but if you'd like to stay a little while and talk to me while I drink my tea–' she broke off abruptly.

With a faintly bewildered look at her, he went across to the armchair in front of the fire and sat down.

He failed utterly to understand her; he'd never really understood what went on behind all that cool, sculptured beauty, he decided. There had been times when he had held her perfect body, trembling and responsive in his arms, and had felt her like a restive young colt straining to be given its head, ending in a wild, mad gallop. On these few occasions, he had been afraid he might not be able to satisfy her. His nervous tension had made a fiasco of what was normally a fairly satisfactory physical relationship.

There was something both proud and fastidious in John's nature which put a permanent rein on his behaviour with his wife. He had never been sure of her; never completely certain that she loved him. At times, he had been convinced that she didn't love him at all and he retired into his shell and was silent and morose for days. Then some word or gesture from Miranda would make him feel better and wonder once again if he had misjudged her.

This uncertainty had clouded his marriage; he could not accept passion for its own sake. A man of high ideals, he wanted his wife's body only if it were given with love. Being perfectly in control of his own physical appetites, he never imposed himself

118

on her. So he waited for her to show that she wanted him in her bed.

During the six years of their marriage, this unspoken arrangement had worked fairly satisfactorily. But now he felt out of his depth. How was it possible that she had voluntarily separated from him, then, without a word of explanation, returned home, and to all appearances was inviting him to a reconciliation?

'John, did you really have me followed?'

Her quietly-spoken question startled him and he flushed uncomfortably. He was a little ashamed of having hired that private detective. At the time, it had seemed sensible because he *HAD* to know if she was planning to leave him. What she did not seem to realize was that he truly loved her; that quiet and restrained though he might always have been, deep within him he was a passionate man, capable of violent emotions and extreme jealousy.

She took his lack of denial for assent.

'Do you want a divorce?' she asked quickly.

'No!'

The retort was instantaneous but even as the words left John's lips he was no longer sure of himself. In a way, he had been happy in his marriage. But in another way it had been incomplete. He would never have been the first to suggest a separation but, on the other hand, now that he knew Miranda was so dissatisfied as his wife, he was not sure he could settle down again and be moderately content. There were other women – Mrs Van de Haal for instance – who obviously found him attractive. It had been a pleasant change to be in the company of a woman who made it plain she thought him wonderful! She had touched his vanity maybe, but was that such a bad thing? A man liked to be admired, to have a woman around who pandered to his wishes and admired rather than criticized him.

'Shall we – try again?' Miranda's voice was hesitant – even shy.

John drew in his breath.

'That's entirely up to you, Miranda. It was you who felt our marriage to be unsatisfactory. If you think you can be happy with me after all, then by all means let's try again.'

This wasn't what she wanted from him. The offer was there but devoid of all the urgency and force that she needed, that she must have to sway her from uncertainty to conviction. If he had only put his arms round her, silence her doubts with kisses, maybe they could have touched again the first exciting moments of their honeymoon. Only as the months had passed, and then the years, had he become so different, so deferential...

'Well?' John's voice was emotionless, without inflexion of any kind. He might have been discussing tomorrow's weather forecast.

'I – I don't know. Perhaps...' she paused, compelled to speak and yet horribly uncertain of herself. 'Do you want to ... to sleep in this room tonight?'

He stared at her across the width of the room, his face white. He wondered if she had any idea how much he would like to make love to her. He knew every curve, every line, every hollow of her beautiful body. He wanted to crush her underneath him, to bury his face against the beauty of her small, pink-tipped breasts and lose himself in purely sensual delight. He wanted the touch of her fingers exploring his face, then their hard, more demanding pressure against his back, her mouth moist and sweet, receiving his. Above all, he wanted to give her everything that was his as a token of love. But not in order to quell some nameless doubt in her mind. No! he refused on principle to use bodily passion in order to solve a mental problem.

He stood up and moved his fingers nervously along the back of a yellow velvet chair.

'This is your home, Miranda. By all means stay here if you wish. But I don't think – well, that sleeping together – can solve anything for either of us. You alone can decide what you want to do. I'm not going to put pressure on you one way or the other. You're not a young girl – you are an intelligent, mature woman. You need no guidance from me.'

'Yes, you're perfectly right!'

He could not know what those words cost her. Pride alone kept her head high, her voice steady, her tone cool.

'Goodnight, John. Thank you for bringing me the tea.'

She stood up, hurried to her dressing table, busying her hands with a comb – a pot of cream – anything so that he should not see the blinding tears in her eyes.

'Goodnight, Miranda,' he said.

When the door closed between them, she flung herself down on the bed, her hands twisting the little frilled pillow. She felt humiliated, defeated. She had wanted to come home – meant to try again to make this marriage work. She had been prepared to take the initiative – to show John that she still needed him, and he had turned her down. Maybe she deserved it. That was not important. All that mattered was that they had failed each other in the moment of crisis and now there was nothing more she could do.

After a while, she undressed and slipped, shivering, between the sheets. She thought over the few hours since her return home, with dull misery. It had gone wrong from the start – the wrong time, the wrong evening engendering the wrong mood in John. It wasn't his fault – but her own, for acting as always on impulse, without thought for possible consequences.

John had called her 'an intelligent, mature woman'. Well, when would she learn to act like one? To use her head instead of her heart as a guide to life? She should have learned by now that her heart was utterly unreliable, leading her from one hopeless, unsatisfactory quest to another. That heart would not help her to find peace of mind or drag her out of shifting sand on to solid rock – the rock of conviction. That wild, unhappy heart had failed tonight to make a new marriage out of the old.

Or was it still drawing her further back – back through the years to her first marriage – to David?

CHAPTER SIX

When Miranda decided to go back to the country home where she had lived as a child, she could not have given anyone a lucid reason for wanting to visit the familiar surroundings. It was simply an instinct to return to the security, the blessed simplicity of that period of her life which had been unexciting, but emotionally uncomplicated.

She booked a room in a small country hotel just outside Hungerford and lunched there alone. As her home was some few miles out of the village she decided to hire a car for the afternoon and drive around in comfort. The hotel manager supplied her with the telephone number of a local car-hire firm. Miranda booked a driver for half past two.

She stepped out of the hotel, neat, elegant in an olive-green perfectly-tailored suit. The black crocodile bag and shoes had been John's Christmas present to her; the Hermes scarf his last birthday present.

The driver came forward to open the door. Miranda looked up to thank him; then frowned thoughtfully. Somewhere, she had seen this man before. He was not wearing chauffeur's uniform but a rather well-cut grey suit, white shirt and wine silk tie. Over it was a short Jaeger coat. He didn't look like a driver – he was far too well-dressed, she thought.

He had recognized her, too, for he said, smiling:

'Why, *Mandy!*'

At once she knew him and the pleased colour came into her pale face. This was Harry, of course. Her mind winged back to the small boy who had so often befriended her in childhood. His father had been her parents' chauffeur-gardener. She and Harry were not supposed to play together.

She studied the man before her with interest. He must be about thirty-five, she realized. Gone was the rather thin, angular boy with the thick, light-brown curls and freckled face. In his place was a pleasant-looking, sturdy man; upright, quite attractive.

When she was five years old, Harry had been seven – Miranda had been unable to give him anything more than hero-worship at a distance. She would lean from her nursery window watching him scale up the old walnut tree like a small brown monkey and long desperately to be allowed to play with him. In the summer, she saw him riding across the field on top of a hay cart, his freckled face happy and smiling, his clothes torn and grubby. She could hear him whistling.

At seven, she still hero-worshipped him and her curiosity had been deepened by an explanation from her governess that Harry was 'Unsuitable' as a playmate for her; he was 'Working-class'; he was 'Inferior'. To satisfy her childish curiosity the governess explained that 'inferior' meant 'beneath' or 'not as good as'. Miranda failed to understand. Harry was far superior to her in every way – he could climb trees, ride a bike, help with the harvest; he knew the names of all the butterflies and how to train a ferret, how to mend a puncture, how a car-engine worked. Miranda knew because she had disobeyed the rule never to play with Harry and had spent several afternoons talking to him behind the potting-shed on her governess's day out.

She liked Harry. After the first shyness, he seemed to like her. Both knew they should not be 'friends' but this only lent their infrequent meetings an added spice. He told her everything he had learned about the countryside and she told him about her more sheltered life; a pantomime she had been to; what it was like learning to play the piano. That interested Harry. He was crazy about music. Once, in exchange for allowing her to hold his ferret, she carried an old HMV portable gramophone down to the potting-shed and let him play records. They stuffed a pair of blue overalls down the loud-speaker so the grown-ups wouldn't hear.

This curious, secret friendship continued through the rather confined and lonely years of Miranda's childhood. As she matured, she began to understand the differences in their social status. From Harry's stories about his home, she learned that there were never any luxuries in a family of eight; what it meant to have jam without butter on your bread; how he and his friends sometimes stole fruit from the neighbouring farm and ate it when they were hungry. There was no such thing for Harry as regular pocket-money. He was lucky to get an ice-cream or lollipop.

Of course, she began to smuggle such delicacies to him which he would only accept in exchange for a service he could do for her. He made her a complete and beauti-ful set of furniture for her dolls-house, which she dared not take back into the house since there was no way of explaining its presence without revealing her friendship with Harry.

Looking back now over the past, it amazed Miranda to realize that during those ten years, no-one had ever known about their secret meetings.

'Why, Harry!' she exclaimed now.

He smiled down at her. His face was still freckled, the warm blue eyes still laughing and full of friendliness.

'I'll sit in the front with you!' Miranda said. 'What a lovely surprise.'

He helped her in and climbed in beside her, then drove away from the hotel. It was a cool, April day of scurrying cloud and a wind that shook the blossom from the almond trees and scattered the pink petals on the ground. She had always loved the silver rivers and broad green pastureland of Berkshire. She gave a sudden sigh of content – of nostalgic enjoyment of this hour.

'The car was ordered for Mrs Villiers. I never for a moment imagined it could be *you*.' He gave a quick sideways glance. 'I recognized you at once. You really haven't changed – what is it? Eighteen years?'

He had a more cultured voice than she would have expected. He was not recognisable as the village boy of the past. Only his hands were a giveaway – big, broad, freckled with short-cut nails.

'It *can't* be as long as that!' Miranda said, laughing. 'It makes me feel so ancient!'

'You don't look it. If you don't mind me telling you, you're a good deal more beautiful than you were as a small girl and you were mighty pretty, even then. I've often wondered how you'd look now.'

'Then you thought about me sometimes?' Miranda asked with feminine curiosity, and not a little touched, too.

'Yes – more than you'd imagine,' he said, a trifle gruffly.

She noted again that his former Berkshire accent was almost non-existent. The years had turned Harry into quite a polished, self-assured man. Her governess might have had difficulty today deciding his social status!

'Look, Mandy, where did you want to go? I'm driving along this road without direction.'

'I wanted to go home, Harry,' Miranda said. 'I was curious to see the old house and grounds after all these years. Oh, I *am* glad you turned up like this. I can't think of anyone in the whole world I'd rather go home with!'

He swung the car into a lane, and looking with pleasure at his profile she saw the colour flush into his healthy face.

'I'm glad, too. I've so often hoped we might meet again. I wanted to thank you.'

'Thank *me?* Whatever for, Harry?'

Suddenly he stopped the car, and for a moment, stared reflectively at the bending branches of the silver-birch wood on their right. Then he said:

'Now I've finally got the chance, I want to get this off my chest, if you don't mind.'

Puzzled, she looked up at him and pushed back the gold bracelet on her left wrist. The pleasant jingle fascinated him – like her beautiful, manicured nails; they were not the grubby little hands of a small girl now.

'What is it you want to say, Harry?'

'A great many things. You see, you changed my whole life, Mandy. But for you, I'd probably be what Dad was in the old days. You gave me the idea of bettering myself in a big way. I've got on in the world – I own quite a nice little business and I have a nice home, money in the bank – a position I'd never have held but for your influence.'

Miranda still did not entirely follow his train of thought. She hadn't seen him since she was fifteen. What lasting influence could she have had on Harry?

Suddenly, he grinned at her.

'You still frown in the same way when you don't understand what I'm talking about!' he teased. 'Remember when I tried to explain how your rabbit had young ones? I don't think you had a clue as to what I was talking about.'

Miranda laughed now, amusedly.

'You forget how "carefully" I was brought up. And I was only about ten at that time.'

'At ten, *my* kind knew all the facts of life! When I was a kid I used to be quite appalled by your innocence. At seventeen...' he broke off and drew in a breath of cigarette smoke.

'Well?' Miranda prompted.

'At seventeen, I realized that your innocence was your protection. I suppose you didn't realize it, but I was madly in love with you. You were a sort of princess to me. I used to call you that in my mind. I worshipped the ground you walked on, Mandy – literally. When you went away I thought I'd never be happy again. I wouldn't eat and you know the appetite *I* had. Mum couldn't understand why I went all morose and mooned around like a lost soul.'

'I never knew.'

'No, of course you didn't. You were still a schoolgirl. And even if you'd known, what difference could it have made. You lived in a different world from mine.'

She tried to remember. She could see Harry as that tall, freckled youth of seventeen – immensely strong, capable, *safe*. His voice was a man's voice and yet to her he had still been just Harry, her secret childhood chum.

He looked at her wryly now.

'Why should you remember? I wasn't all that important to you except as a playmate. You began to grow up – go to concerts, learning "culture" I suppose it was called. You hadn't much time for me at the end. But I remember, Mandy. I remember every little tiny thing about you. Because of you, I decided to make something of myself. Because of you, I worked like the devil at school. I surprised myself and everyone else by passing exams I'd never have bothered about but for you. I went on to technical college, studied at nights, bought *books* and read them, and got an engineering diploma. When I wasn't studying, I worked at the local garage, learning more about cars and machines. I saved what I earned and by the time I was twenty-five I was able to buy the garage – lock stock and barrel. I began to build up the business – get an assistant – and now, well, now I have two hundred and thirty men working for me in various branches all over Berkshire. I have several garages and hire-firms. There's a car-sales side to the business, the hire side, maintenance, and a few years ago I branched out into agricultural machinery. I've got all the money I want – the kind of life I want.'

'It's wonderful, Harry. A real Success Story,' she said, feeling the old journalist's interest stir in her. The newspapers loved stories of men who made good and rose from nothing. 'But I still don't see how *I*...' she paused.

He gave her a twisted smile.

'No! It'll sound mad to you but when I started on this ladder to success, I dreamed that one day I might meet you again – on *your* level. I thought maybe you'd see me differently then – that maybe you would – oh, hell, it seems crazy even to me today, but I thought I might one day be in a position to ask you to marry me.'

She was too astounded to speak. He seemed calm, yet when she put out a hand and covered his where it gripped the steering wheel, she could feel it shaking and knew that he was moved emotionally. It was all so unexpected – so staggering – but inevitably the female in her was stirred and flattered. Harry, dear Harry was a success – and still in love with his dream of *her*.

'Of course I grew up – I read somewhere that you'd got married and that was that,' he went on. 'I suppose I might have given up the struggle then but after all those years I couldn't. I still had to make the grade, make myself what I thought you'd like me to be. Remember how you used to correct my grammar?'

'No, I didn't surely!' Miranda said, horrified. 'What a beastly little prig I must have been.'

'No, you weren't. I asked you to tell me. I don't suppose you remember.' He grinned disarmingly. 'You gave me a standard to live up to. But for you, I'd have stayed where I was.'

'You've been marvellous,' she said with genuine admiration. 'And you're happy now, Harry?'

'*You* define happiness for me, Mandy, and I'll answer your question.'

He started up the engine and let in the clutch. Miranda stared at the man beside her. What an incredible person he had become. How frightening to realize how even as a child one could influence another person without being aware of it. Harry had turned himself into a successful business-man because he'd once been in love, in his adolescent fashion, with her!

She glanced at him again, seeing him for the first time as an equal, a possible 'boy-friend'. She admitted that he had great attraction. The frank, honest face with its boyish freckles was disarming and somehow touching. His blue eyes were fringed with very dark lashes. His mouth was wide and humorous. He looked gentle, yet at the same time strong and very masculine. He was broad-shouldered, his tall body narrow-ing down to long legs which she suddenly recalled, were always covered with scars and bruises when he was a child.

He turned to her again.

'Tell me about yourself, Mandy. It's your turn.'

'Not now! We're nearly home,' Miranda said, pointing to the long high stone wall which they were now skirting. When they came to a giant walnut tree, she added: 'Look, Harry, *your* tree. Oh, I wonder who is living in the house now. Do you think they'd let us go in? Turn into the drive and let's ask.'

He swung the car round and drove through open wrought-iron gates into a sweeping drive. At the end of it they came to a grey stone house, covered in creeper and looking rather forlorn and deserted. The garden was full of tulips half-choked by weeds.

'Some people called Inchliff used to live here, but I heard they went abroad,' Harry informed her. 'The daughter got married to an American, and the parents went over to stay with her, so they say.'

He pulled up outside the house and Miranda said:

'Is it up for sale? There's no board.'

'Yes – I saw one by the gate. Let's go back and make sure.'

The 'For Sale' sign and the address of agents in Hungerford was fixed to the left of one of the gate-posts. Harry said:

'I know the agents. Shall we go and ask for the key?'

'Yes, lets!' Miranda felt suddenly happy and even excited. Harry had always had a wonderful aptitude for anticipating her wishes. It was really a piece of luck his coming to drive her today. She knew now that he would never have done so but that a 'flu epidemic had made them short of drivers, so 'the boss' had stepped into the breach.

Half an hour later, they came back from Hungerford with the keys.

'I felt rather naughty pretending I might want to buy Friars House!' Miranda said, smiling. 'The Agents were obviously so anxious to have it off their hands.'

'Not surprised!' Harry said, as he slipped the key in the lock. 'It's been empty for quite a time, the chap was telling me. Far too big for most people, and I gather the furniture is pretty old-fashioned.'

He took her arm and unlocked the front door. They went into the hall. It was very bleak and chilly and Miranda looked round and shivered. It was all so familiar, yet so strange. Smaller, less magnificent than she had imagined.

'Not so sure I want to be here after all!' she said in a low voice.

Harry laughed.

'Empty houses are always a bit depressing. Look, that was your father's study.'

'How do you know?' Miranda asked. 'You never once came into the house!'

'Your father gave me a thrashing in there – the day I took you fishing.'

'He *what?*'

Harry laughed.

'You didn't know, but someone saw us and told him. After he'd thrashed me, he tried to make me promise never to take you fishing again. I think he was terrified you might have fallen in and drowned. I said I'd only promise if *he* promised not to punish you, too. Quite a decent chap, your father. I think he wanted to give me another six for being cheeky, then he laughed and tossed me half-a-crown and gave me his word he wouldn't punish you.'

'Oh, Harry. He never told me.'

'Well, he couldn't. As a man of honour, if he'd let you know he knew, he'd have had to punish you, wouldn't he? At least, that's the way I figured it out at the time. Let's go upstairs.'

Miranda only glanced briefly into her mother's old bedroom – it 'gave her the creeps' she decided. The other bedrooms on the second floor disturbed her less. But in the west wing of the house she looked around more curiously. Here was her day and night nursery. The bars were still across the windows. Here, too, was her governess's room and the maids' bedrooms. They, too, seemed so much smaller than she remembered them. To a child's eye a little space must seem vast – just as young adults appeared old.

She stood beside Harry, looking out of the dormer window of her bedroom and across the overgrown garden to the potting-shed.

'I'd forgotten till this moment how lonely I used to feel,' she said suddenly, her throat aching. 'I used to pray every night to God to send me a brother or sister. After a while, I gave up praying. Then I had *you*...'

He stood there watching her, his eyes warm and intent.

'Then I did mean *something* to you?'

'A lot, a lot!' Miranda cried truthfully. 'You were my only friend, Harry.'

'I can hardly believe that.'

'But you were. My parents asked the children from the big houses in the area – children of their friends – and I went to their parties. We just stood around playing with expensive toys or eyeing each other like critical adults – rather nastily, really – and then we'd sit down to a huge tea and some of us were sick and the others bored, and only one or two of the high-spirited really seemed to enjoy themselves. I didn't happen to be one. I just looked forward to getting back home and seeing you.'

'But why?' he asked, amazed.

'Because you were my *friend*,' she repeated the word, stressing it. 'We spoke the same language.'

Harry's brows went up quizzically.

'Hardly. You were Miss Miranda. I was just the gardener's boy.'

'I never thought of myself as Miss Miranda where you were concerned and you never called me "Miss".'

'That's true,' he said.

She went to the window and looked down. The wind was getting up – the sharp, cold wind of spring, swaying the heads of tulips and the long lanky weeds that had been allowed to grow too high. She could see the wrought-iron well-head, half hidden by a bramble that had run wild. She could remember playing with Harry down there after dark one summer's evening when she had stolen out to meet him. Miss Emily had thought she was safely settled in the schoolroom reading. But she had knelt in the dusk beside Harry, and they each had a fistful of stones and dropped them one by one into the well and wondered how far they sank as they listened to each 'plop'. Once Harry had threatened to climb into the old bucket and get her to turn the handle and let him down, but she had put both arms around him and dragged him back from the stone parapet.

She turned now to ask Harry if he remembered this incident and how sick with fear she had been. He had forgotten, but memory revived. Yes, he recalled that look of terror in her eyes. He could even feel the straining of her thin, childish arms, and hear her voice:

'No, you're not to, Harry. You'll fall in and be drowned and I'll never see you again. And I'll fall in, too, trying to save you.'

It had been the threat to her life, not to his, that had held him back.

'You were a little bit fond of me. I treasure all those memories, Mandy.'

The moment was emotionally nostalgic. Her eyes filled with tears.

She turned away from the window and stood face to face with him. They were so close that although their bodies were not touching, it was almost an embrace. She raised her eyes and looking into his, saw with a moment of both surprise and dismay that the friendly, teasing expression had vanished from them. He was looking at her now with quite a different expression – one of love and pain and longing.

Suddenly, his arms were round her. She could feel the trembling of his long, muscular body.

'Mandy, Mandy – forgive me. You've grown so lovely. You look, sort of lost! It hurts me.'

She hid her face on his shoulder but he put out a hand and tilted her chin upwards, so that he could look into her eyes.

'What is it? What's wrong? Why aren't you happy? In the car you told me nothing. You're married. Wasn't it a success?'

She didn't know what to reply, or if he really expected an answer to such questions. A moment later his lips were hard against her own and as if she had entered a sudden ecstatic dream she felt herself relax and respond, slowly at first then with growing abandon as his hands slid down her back to her waist.

'Mandy, Mandy, Mandy!'

Between kisses he uttered her name over and over again. They were both trembling now. She began to feel afraid of the tension that vibrated from him – communicating itself to her.

She called a sudden halt.

'Harry, don't – please, *please!*'

He released her at once, so suddenly that she almost lost her balance.

'I'm sorry!' he said harshly. 'Terribly sorry! I apologize.'

She stepped forward and caught his arm and laid her cheek against his shoulder. Beneath it she could feel the jolting rhythm of his powerful heart-beats.

'Don't apologize, Harry. I'm not sorry. It's just – well, just that ... my life is in such a muddle and I am so confused...'

'Would you like me to drive you back to the hotel?'

She shook her head.

'No!'

He was only just gaining command of himself again. The violence, the significance of their sudden embrace had unnerved him. He had never dreamed it possible that he would ever kiss Miranda and certainly not like *that*. There was an intoxication on her lips which no man could resist. He had lost his head completely.

'Shall I take you somewhere else?' His voice was formal, polite.

'Harry, don't be hurt. I ... I wish there were somewhere we could talk. It's so cold here.'

At once he relaxed and came close to her

again in spirit.

'I saw some wood and coal downstairs. We *could* light a fire down there, or up here if you prefer it.'

'I'd like that – but suppose someone sees smoke coming out of the chimney?'

'They won't – and even if they did, we could say we were trying out the chimney-draught for you.'

Miranda felt a quick wave of excitement sweep through her. It was almost as if she were a child again, planning some forbidden escapade with her friend, Harry.

'All right!'

While he was downstairs getting the fuel, she glanced around her again. The familiar furnishings of her own childhood had gone but the room must still have been used as a room for older children. There was an old sofa along one wall, a large unvarnished oak table with four wooden chairs tucked under it; a bookcase piled with various school textbooks and storybooks and an encyclo-paedia piled into it haphazardly. The atmos-phere smelled faintly of ink, and damp. On the floor was a rather threadbare faded blue carpet – stained – torn; and on the mantel-piece was a nursery clock and a vase with crêpe-paper flowers in it – dusty and faded.

'We ought not to be here!' Miranda thought and then, hearing Harry's voice calling from the stairs, she gave a sudden happy laugh. It was fun. She hadn't been young and silly for such a long, long while.

Harry came in, his arms full of paper, firewood and logs. He knelt down and with his usual efficiency soon had a good fire blazing.

Miranda knelt down beside him and spread her numbed fingers to the flames. He put his large hands over hers and began to rub them gently until the circulation was restored.

'Better?'

She nodded, and moved way from the fire to the sofa. Harry sat down beside her.

'Now, please tell me about yourself,' he said.

Very briefly, she outlined her life with David and how she had lost her baby.

'I married again some years afterwards,' she told Harry. 'Now – well, I've separated from my present husband – not legally, but I wanted time to sort myself out.'

Harry looked bewildered.

'I guessed from your face you weren't happy, but I can't understand it. You always seemed to me destined for a story-book ending – you know "Happily-ever-after". Perhaps that is because you were my Fairy Princess and that's the way fairy stories end.'

'*Should* end!' Miranda said, bitterly. 'But in real life, it isn't always the case. What about you? Has there been a girl in your life?'

He looked away from her out of the dusty window at the clouded sky. It was beginning to rain. Only the pleasant crackle of the burning firewood lightened the gloom.

'I married about ten years ago. I have two children, a boy and a girl – Will and Ann.'

'Did you marry a local girl?'

'Yes, you knew her,' he said. 'You remember Gracie?'

'Gracie?' she repeated, vaguely, then: 'Good lord, yes, Gracie Woodfall. The dentist's child.'

He nodded. His face was stern – curiously sad.

'She was rather a pretty little girl – fair hair, very shy.'

'That's Gracie. She's still a bit shy. I thought I could change that, but I didn't succeed. I think I fell for her because she was fair and slim – and reminded me of you,' he said.

She felt a lump in her throat.

'Oh, Harry,' she said sadly, 'aren't you happy?'

'I told you earlier to define happiness for me before I could answer that question!' Then he said more seriously: 'For the most part, I'm content. Gracie loves me. She's a good wife and a good mother. We just aren't lovers. But our children – well, we think they're fine. We have most things we need. It's just...' he broke off for a moment and then added, harshly:

'I was never really in love with Gracie. I think she knows it, although we don't ever discuss it. She takes things for granted. But I don't. You're the only girl I've ever really loved, Mandy. No, don't interrupt me – let me finish. There may never be another chance to tell you and I want you to know. You have never been far away from my thoughts all these years. If I had a decision to make, I would find myself saying: "What would Mandy have thought best?" Without knowing it, you've helped me to choose my house, names for my children; you've helped me to solve numerous problems. I've always fought against this subconscious need to refer to you because I know it isn't fair to Gracie. I suppose it became such a habit in my childhood, I just couldn't get out of it.'

Miranda was still shivering, although the temperature in the room was rising.

'You frighten me, Harry. It makes me feel you might have been far happier if we'd never been friends as children.'

He caught her arms in a sudden violent grip.

'Don't say that – don't ever even *think* it, Mandy. I owe everything I am to you. *I'm* not sorry, so why should you be? No one achieves everything they want in this life and I gave up my romantic notions of winning my Princess many years ago. I can't help it if part of me still belongs to you – and always will. I accept it.'

Silence fell between them. Without realizing it they held hands again – their fingers interlocked. Miranda felt a complexity of emotions. She could not help but be flattered by such a deathless devotion. At the same time, she felt a deep pity for Harry. Had he been born into different circumstances, with different parents, it might all have been so different. Had he been the child of one of her parents' many friends, he would have come to the house to play with her. Later, it would have been accepted that he should take her out to parties and dances. No doubt a romance between them would have been encouraged. But there had never been any hope of that. She had known his worth, taken him for what he was, and loved him. But if he had ever spoken of his love when she was in her late teens or twenties, would her childish devotion have deepened to adult love?

'I can't help being very sorry!' she said at last. 'It all seems so unfair.'

'I don't see why!'

'Because now, when it's all too late, you can't reap the rewards of all your efforts, Harry. There is no more hope of achieving what you worked for now, than there was a long time ago.'

'You mean marriage to you? No, I know that,' he said grimacing. 'But you did kiss me, Mandy – you returned my kiss. I felt all the wonder and magic of you in my arms.'

She felt suddenly humbled. A kiss – such a small, meaningless thing! She had given so much more to other men in her life – men like Alastair, perhaps, who had taken it for granted, and her body, too; men who had never adored her all their lives – as Harry had done.

'Harry!' It was half question, half statement.

An instant later she was in his arms and he was kissing her again. There was no practised sensuality in the pressure of his mouth – only a gentle giving which hardened into a desperate hungry longing.

He drew his lips away and buried his face in her hair.

'Oh, my God, Mandy! I never believed I would really hold you in my arms. You can't know what it means to me. You mustn't hate me for being disloyal to Gracie – this is something quite separate from what's between Gracie and me. Mandy, I love you. I'll always love you, Princess.'

There was nothing in her heart that could equal his feeling for her; but she had a deep affection for him – a child's loyalty and a woman's stirring pity. She put up a hand and stroked his cheek gently as if trying to soothe him. She was not afraid of him. She trusted him completely – a trust rooted in the memories of their childhood. He would do nothing to offend or upset her – nothing against her will. But she could sense his deep passionate longing. She was held so tightly that she felt the hard urgent body against hers, and was astonished by the warmth of her growing response.

He wants me! she thought. Why not? It would mean so much to him ... and to me?

It would be an act of disloyalty to John. It would be committing adultery; breaking her vows. Strangely enough, in spite of the number of men in her life, she had never yet done that. But she tried now to argue with herself. John had rejected her – refused her offer to him to share her bed. Why shouldn't she give Harry the physical satisfaction he craved and which John had not wanted? To Harry it would mean the fulfilment of his whole life's dream.

There were tears in her eyes as she put her hands either side of his face and turned it towards her. She could see now the desperate, tortured expression in his eyes.

'It's all right, Harry,' she whispered. 'It's all right!'

For a moment, he gazed down at her unbelievingly and then, seeing this was on her part an act of surrender willingly made, he buried his face against her breast. He gave a kind of moan.

'Oh, Mandy darling; oh, darling; oh, my God!'

He helped her out of her jacket and shirt with a tenderness, an exquisite gentleness she had never received from any other lover. He began to kiss her naked shoulders and then her breasts. Slowly, as he undressed her she felt her own body stir with something more than pity – with a hot, answering desire. When at last she saw his strong, naked body, she realized that it was not to be all giving on her part. It was also to be a taking. She watched him move cushions from sofa to floor in front of the glowing log fire and he seemed to her beautifully proportioned; and beautiful, too, in the aesthetic sense with his broad shoulders, his strong legs and rippling muscles. He was like a Michelangelo statue silhouetted against the firelight.

When he came back towards her, his face was soft with love and desire. He picked her up and carried her effortlessly across the room. Then he lay down beside her on the hearth-rug and began to kiss every part of her cool body. She clung to him and caressed him in return until they became one sculptured, perfect statue of primitive man and woman in the act of love.

When it was all over, she lay quiet in his arms. She felt no guilt, no remorse – only a quiet satisfaction of body and mind, and a deep half-buried sadness because it was all over now and could never happen again. In its way the sudden unplanned moments of shared passion with Harry was unequalled in her life's experience.

He lay without moving – face against her breast, eyes closed.

'I shall never forget this, Mandy, never, *never!*' he whispered.

She traced the line of his mouth with one finger and said thoughtfully:

'Harry, you won't let it spoil anything between you and Gracie? I may seem inconsistent after what I've just done but I wouldn't want to come between you and your wife.'

He shook his head.

'No there's no question of that. It never *has* been this way with Gracie – never could be. It isn't only her fault – it's mine, too. For Gracie, sex was always from the start a rather unfortunate necessity. So you see ... this – this joy, this perfection you've shown me are beyond compare, and belong to you and me only.'

She understood. It was the same with her. It was a strange, unique union – all the more poignant by virtue of the fact that they had known and loved each other in their childish innocence. Poor, poor Harry. And poor Gracie. What she had missed, if she could never appreciate what a wonderful lover her husband could be!

'I know I'll never see you again, Mandy. In a way, I suppose you'll regard this as a crazy sort of romantic episode. But I'm glad. It has been such a revelation for me. I don't want anything ever to spoil it.'

'You don't think it could be the same if we repeated it?' Miranda asked in a curious, unemotional way.

'Might be – who can say? Your mood, my mood, our future actions could all go wrong. I couldn't bear to risk spoiling this memory. You said earlier that I had never had any reward – well, now I've had it, darling – all I've ever wanted and far more than I ever believed would be mine.'

She was in tears then. And he kissed and comforted her, as he might have done in their childhood, telling her not to cry.

They dressed slowly, at ease with each other, sad and yet content. They replaced the cushions, and made sure the fire was out. They realized that time had flown and they had been together for five happy hours. Like two old friends on excellent terms they left the house, arm in arm. Back at her hotel, she suggested that Harry should go in and have a drink with her in the nearly empty bar.

They sat together, drinking gin and tonic; talking like friends who have long been separated and have much to discuss. Harry did not refer to the past again. In the hearing of the barman they were conventional – adopted an impersonal attitude – laughing sometimes over a shared joke. But now and again their eyes met in a long deep look of mutual understanding – of grief perhaps – that this must be a final parting. The 'poor little rich girl' and the gardener's boy who had grown up and for a few hours had shared the sharpest ecstasy of intimate loving and giving – but would never see each other again.

When he glanced at his wrist-watch and said he must be off, Miranda went out with him to the car.

He held her for a brief moment in the darkness. As he kissed her good-bye she sensed his pain and reluctance to leave her. She clung to him for a moment but not wishing to make the parting harder, finally drew away from him. She said softly:

'Good-bye, Harry – darling Harry. I'll never forget you. Thank you for loving me.'

She stood quietly in the cold night air watching the red light of his car grow smaller and fainter until it disappeared into the blackness of the night. Then she turned back to the hotel.

Once more, Miranda was utterly alone.

CHAPTER SEVEN

Miranda lay on her bed in the hotel, arms crossed behind her head and tried not to think of Harry. The sooner she left the hotel, the happier he would be. At the same time, she found it hard not to keep thinking about the strange, unexpected pleasure of the afternoon. It was marred only by the knowledge that she had been unfaithful to John and, worst of all, that she had enjoyed it. This seemed to matter more than the infidelity itself. It worried her, too, to know that John's hold on her was so slight that it could be broken by a few fleeting hours of passion. Harry had never before existed for her as a man to love or be loved in that way. The boy she had hero-worshipped as her only true friend, had become her lover only through pity and shared passion and to stay here where she might easily run into him again would be a mistake. Harry, himself, would prefer the whole thing to end here and now.

She lay quiet, wondering what to do next. No more visits to past loves – that much was certain. Suddenly she sat upright with a pleasant start of anticipation. She would ring

Sue and Peter. She had not seen them for several months. Sue was one of her dearest friends…

Sue answered the phone. Immediately she heard Miranda's voice and having no particular plans, she invited Miranda to stay at the flat.

'Come at once tomorrow, if you can. We're only here for three more days and then we're off to Italy.'

'I'll come now!'

Miranda packed the following morning and took a train to London. She was pleased to see the familiar penthouse and found Sue unchanged. She was a little plumper but still the same cheerful, hard-working journalist Patrick had liked so much and whom Peter, her husband, adored. Miranda had always envied them their unity. Their marriage had really made each of them complete – more fully themselves and yet an essential part of each other.

'No need to ask if you're still happy!' Miranda said as Sue gave her a drink and watched Miranda unpack in the tiny spare room. 'Peter, of course, is on top of the world, too.'

Sue nodded happily.

'We're off to Italy for a fortnight. It hardly seems possible after all the planning and saving. Just think, Mandy, no horrible, chilly April weather for two whole weeks!'

She sat puffing a cigarette while Miranda put on a dressing-gown and lay under the eiderdown – enjoying the complete relaxation in the friendly, congenial atmosphere.

'How's John?' asked Sue.

'Oh, he's well. We ... Sue, I'd rather not go into it all now but we've separated for a while.'

Sue's cheerful face creased into a look of genuine concern.

'Oh, darling, I *am* sorry.'

'We may get back together again in time – I don't know. I just need to be away from him for a while to sort myself out.'

'What do you plan to do then? Are you writing? Working?'

Miranda shook her head.

'Neither! As you know, I gave up journalism when I married John. As to the novels – well, there didn't seem to be much to write about – or perhaps that is just an excuse. Maybe I lack the incentive. In the old days, I needed money. That helped me to work.'

Sue grinned and nodded.

'I always forget you're so filthy rich these days, Mandy. If you can afford it and you have nothing else to do, why not come to Italy with Peter and me?'

'But I can't possibly...' Mandy began and then thought: *'Why not? I've nothing else to do. Why don't I go?'*

'Mandy, *do* come. You know Peter would

love to have you along. He likes you best of all my girl friends and I think it would be terrific. *Do*, Mandy, please!'

'It's sweet of you to suggest it, but I don't want to spoil things for you and Peter. After all, three's a crowd.'

Sue laughed.

'Nonsense! We're not a honeymoon couple. We've been married fourteen years. And even if we do want the odd evening to ourselves, I know you well enough to be sure you'd fade tactfully on such occasions. Remember when we all three went on that tour to Le Touquet one Easter week-end? Peter always says it was the best holiday we ever had.'

Miranda knit her brows – remembering.

'H'm. You two were just engaged. I was supposed to be the chaperon!'

'And a jolly tactful one you were, too. Mandy, do come to Italy. Have you got a passport. We've still got a couple of days to fix everything up. We're going to spend the first two nights in Rome, to see the sights, then we're taking a hired car to Siena. Every-one says it is gorgeous. Peter wants to see the fantastic buildings and we can share the expenses of a hired car which we'll pick up in Rome.'

The idea began to grow in appeal to Miranda. She had nothing else to do, and this would give her the complete change of scene she needed. With Sue and Peter she could relax completely and the thought of seeing Rome and Siena, and all the historic beauties with them was very tempting. She'd been to Italy before with John – to Florence and Capri. John had never been particularly interested in art galleries and architecture although he had generously put aside two days to escort her round the places she had wished to see. But Sue and Pete were as beauty conscious and interested in classic painting, as Miranda. Now they could browse round churches, and sit in the Sistine Chapel for hours without fear of boring anyone else.

It wasn't very long before Miranda gave in and promised to join them if Peter had no objection.

Peter was quite a bit older than Sue. His hair was beginning to recede and get thin on top; his rather delicate face was lined. But the creases round the nice hazel eyes had been etched by laughter. He was one of the best-tempered men Miranda had ever met. Sue was jolly and amiable, too. Perhaps, Miranda thought enviously, much of their happiness in marriage was due to the sense of humour that these two always shared. It was so much more important than all John's wealth.

They set off for Rome in fine spirits. Their

flight from Heathrow was trouble-free and Miranda felt better already. It was good to leave England and all the troubles behind her.

They travelled tourist class in the Comet. As this was a cheaper rate, three seats had been put in in place of the usual two in the first-class cabin, and so they were able to sit together. Peter sat between the two women. He was attentive and considerate – never leaving Miranda out of any of the fun or friendliness.

A pretty, dark air hostess served them an excellent cold lunch. Miranda, who was more used to travelling first-class with her rich husband, told her friends that this form of travel seemed to lack only the free champagne; otherwise everything was the same and just as comfortable.

The flight was over in a miraculously short time. Soon they were touching down at Rome Airport. The new building seemed to them all to be like a vast palace of glass – crowded and noisy – pandemonium, in fact, but exciting.

As the tall, lovely English girl passed through the Customs with her friends, the eyes of not one but many Italian officials followed the graceful figure with open admiration. She looked good; she knew it. This morning, leaving London with Sue and Peter she had felt her fatigue and depression fade away. She knew that her eyes were shining and her heart was lighter. As they entered the bus that was to take them to the Rome Air Terminal, she felt a sense of anticipation. She smiled at the handsome conductor and returned his greeting.

They stayed at a small hotel in a one-way street at the top of the Spanish Steps.

Miranda's sight was at once caught by the beauty of those splendid and famous steps. The flower-women sat there beside their great baskets of delicate spring blossoms. Peter, at once brought large bunches of Parma violets; gave one to Miranda and one to his wife. As she buried her face in them and inhaled their fresh spring scent, Miranda was unexpectedly reminded of the violets David had given to her. In those early days of their marriage, there'd been no money to spare for expensive flowers but whenever he saw a shop or flower-stall selling them, he always bought her violets. There had been a huge armful of them the day Melanie was born...

She shivered and closed her mind swiftly to such memories.

It was a warm, golden morning in Rome – like summer at home. Miranda gloried in it. Rome was all and more than all she had imagined – a truly magnificent city. Seen from the top of the Spanish Steps she caught a glimpse of the many church spires and towers, grey and carved against the blue sky; felt the blessed warmth of the sun and was unutterably glad that she had 'run away' like this with her friends.

There was so much she wanted to see – the ruins of the Coliseum with its dark history of suffering and savage splendour where one could almost hear the intriguing echo of Roman voices urging their gladiators on to death or cheering the Christian martyrs nearly two-thousand years ago; the modern magnificence of the Sports Stadium and autostradas; the scenes of Mussolini's triumph and downfall. Perhaps most of all she anticipated her first sight of St Peter's Square and the Sistine Chapel.

Peter hired a little Fiat. He drove well and turned out to be one of those geniuses at reading maps. They spent a glorious day. Then Miranda took them to dine at the famous restaurant just behind the Excelsior run by an Englishman named George, and where they had a superb meal washed down by the finest red Italian wine.

But it was the following morning which she always remembered. They drove to Vatican City after parking the little Fiat near St Peter's Square. Miranda was enraptured by the marvellous picture gallery – the Byzantine and Italian Primitives, the Flemish paintings – and all the incredible works by the greatest of Italian masters. Peter knew a lot about them all and was a fine guide. Miranda and Sue had time to pause and examine things without being made to rush by with crowds of Americans and other foreign tourists led by paid lecturers.

When they reached the Sistine Chapel, she was already a little dazed by the wonder of all they had seen. But now the three friends sat down and looked up at the ceiling at the frescoes painted by Michelangelo. Peter pointed out the unearthly work – the history of the world's beginning, the glorious colours Michelangelo had left as a permanent testament to his genius.

After several hours Miranda left the chapel and walked back through the sunlit square to the car again, feeling humbled – even ashamed. What right had she to concentrate on her little personal, petty difficulties in the face of that splendour – that opulence of colour and design?

But Peter soon swung from his own sense of awe to his natural gaiety. He took them out to lunch and before long the old restless craving stirred in Miranda's mind and heart. The lost, lonely woman in her crept back. She wondered if she would find the real and lasting happiness her heart craved.

The next morning they left Rome and set out to Siena. The little car went well. The weather was perfect. The long drive was a joy under a cloudless sky. The Italian spring was truly intoxicating, and this was for all three an initiation into the soft, golden beauty of Tuscany. The countryside was impressive – mile after mile of sweeping hills, deep valleys and olive groves, silver-green in the sun, curving rivers. They passed small, lovely hamlets, clusters of white cottages or pink-washed villas on the crest of the hills, surmounted by the inevitable church.

It was late afternoon when they came to Siena. That to Miranda was an unforgettable experience. The medieval city lay on the heights. Soft, deep-burnt rose in colour, enclosed by a high wall silhouetted sharply against the blue April sky. As they drove through one of the colossal gateways – the immense bronze doors were open to receive them – Miranda said:

'Now I understand why you wanted to come here, Peter, instead of going to Capri or one of the more ordinary coastal resorts. *This* is terrific.'

The streets seemed strangely dim and narrow. The buildings were so high that they cast dark shadows across the cobbles. Miranda had to look way up above her head in order to see the light. All the houses were beautiful; narrow, decorated with wrought-iron balconies and shutters, dominated by the towering cathedral.

'Here you have before you,' said Peter, the architect, 'the finest example, probably in the world, of fourteenth-century Gothic style.'

They had booked into a small hotel near the Campo Square. The Piazza del Campo was one of the places Peter particularly wished to see. Miranda was enchanted by it. Here stood the vast tower of the town hall with its famous clock, which they called the *Palazzo Pubblico;* here was the gay fountain – the *Fonte Gaia;* and the pigeons strutting in hundreds over the stones, fed by the tourists, rising suddenly with a wild flutter of wings up towards the sun. It was a square of splendid ornate, burnt-rose buildings. And here every year the famous *Palio* horse race was run. Miranda wished that she could have seen one but they did not take place until later in the summer.

'We'll have a bit of shut-eye and a bath,' said Peter. 'Then dine at the Cappello Restaurant. I've been told there is a good little bar there and that the food and wine are first-rate.'

It was seven o'clock before they arrived at the Cappello. It was an attractive, underground restaurant where the walls were covered with signed photographs of famous people who at one time or other had visited Siena and sampled the superb wine-cellar. Above it was a hotel but because it was in the centre of the city, Peter had arranged for them to stay in a less crowded part of Siena.

They settled down on stools in the small, intimate bar where there was already a crowd drinking their aperitifs.

Peter turned to Miranda. She looked wonderful, he thought. Already the sun had caught her cheeks. She had dropped years and looked so much better and happier than when he had first seen her at home four days ago. Tonight she wore a chestnut-brown jersey-suit that clung to her lovely figure, a white-silk scarf around her neck. Her hair was sleek and shining. She always managed to look so elegant, he thought. Even in the middle of a fantastic sequestered city like Siena where beauty and magnificence abounded, Miranda's loveliness was still eye-catching.

'What's it to be, Mandy? Gin and Vermouth?'

She nodded.

While he was ordering the drinks, Miranda turned to see if Sue was on her way back from the powder-room. As her glance wandered over the cosmopolitan crowd, her eyes rested for a moment on a dark-haired, striking-looking man who sat with another man at one of the tables. His profile was vaguely familiar. He was outstandingly handsome in a smooth, rather continental way. Puzzled, she was about to look away when the man turned and he looked straight at her.

Across the room, she now saw his expression of astonishment, then delight, and his lips formed her name. A smile crossed his face.

'Why it's *Tony Barrance!*' she thought. He stood up, whispered to his companion, and came straight across the room to her.

'Mandy – Mandy Leyland!' he exclaimed and held out a carefully manicured hand. His dark, heavily-lashed eyes were smiling at her brilliantly.

'Hello, Tony. My name is Villiers now,' she corrected him. 'How are you after all this time?'

'I could hardly believe my eyes when I saw you just now. You'd recognized me already hadn't you?'

'I wasn't absolutely certain. I thought it might be you.'

'Darling, it's a splendid surprise!'

He sounds as if he means it, Miranda thought, and recalled how easily and well Tony could turn on the charm and enthusiasm when it suited him. Briefly, she introduced him to Peter.

'An old friend of mine, Tony Barrance! Tony, this is my friend Peter. He and his wife Sue and I are on holiday here.'

'Let me get you a drink,' Tony said to them both, then seeing they already had them, ordered one for himself. Then he turned back to Miranda.

'This *is* a surprise!' he said again. 'Are you staying in Siena? For how long? We simply must get together and catch up on the years. I've never been to Siena before. It isn't really my cup of tea but my – er – party insisted on stopping here on our way from Florence to Rome. Are you actually staying in this place? I am. How long since we last met, darling? It's amazing running into you.'

Miranda paused before answering. How long? Ten years? She wondered with feminine vanity what he thought of her. Time had been quite kind to him – he was still the handsome debonair playboy; the Peter Pan type who would still look boyish at forty. Yes, he must be nearly that, though beside Peter, he seemed years younger. It was only when one examined the handsome face more closely that one saw the first signs of too much good-living, too much drinking, in the puffiness beneath the eyes; the slackness of the beautifully-shaped mouth and the muscles under the chin.

He was all attention – lighting her cigarette, looking suggestively deeper into her eyes with an intimacy she well remembered.

Same old Tony, she thought, suddenly amused.

He had acquired a perfect technique with women years ago and clearly it must have served him in good stead for he hadn't varied it. That deep, searching look into her eyes, that slight pressure of his hand on her shoulder, or his knee against hers. Without appearing to flirt, he was making it known that he still found her attractive – that their old friendship could revive and go a lot further if she was interested. Yes, Miranda knew it all, she thought and not without bitterness.

Once, she had been completely taken in by Tony – believed he meant all the extravagant things he used to say – felt sure that he said them only to her. But she'd been a lot younger then – a lot less experienced.

She'd met Tony at a lunch-party about a year after Patrick had been flown to hospital in England. Tony was supposed to be partnering their hostess but he paid no attention to the other girl beside him. He had turned to Miranda and concentrated on her.

She had been flattered by the way he monopolized her; amused by his light conversation and obvious admiration. Her heart was still in the hospital, suffering in thought with Patrick, but her mind was entertained by Tony and when he invited her to dine with him that evening, she accepted readily.

Dining in comfort at the Mirabelle, she learned that Tony was in the Foreign Office. His family were in the hunting set, living in Leicestershire. He had his own flat in London. He was widely travelled, a good talker and an amusing companion, so conversation between them didn't flag. Later, they danced cheek-to-cheek and Tony held her just a little too close, his hand pressing against the small of her back. She gave him no encouragement because she had no wish to become emotionally involved while the question of Patrick was still unresolved. Although Patrick had by that time stated quite adamantly that there could never be any question of marriage because he was so hopelessly crippled, Miranda was still uncertain of the future. She hoped it might be possible that some miraculous operation would be performed; even if not, she was prepared to stand by Patrick if he changed his mind and wanted to marry her. During that one short visit to him in hospital, she had been swept with such a fierce pity that she could spare no thought for herself.

But the dinner with Tony was succeeded by lunch the next day, then a day at Henley, race meetings and a *tête-à-tête* dinner at his flat. She began to realize that it was not after all possible to live on pity alone. Her young, active mind craved action as strongly as her body. She was forced to conclude that if she married Patrick, she might fail him. Perhaps a quiet, thoughtful, more dedicate kind of girl could have made the supreme sacrifice – but Miranda knew it was not for her, just as Patrick had known it.

She continued to visit Patrick. Then came the inevitable day when she knew that what had existed between them was over. He even appeared relieved when she told him that she was going out a lot, and casually mentioned Tony. But Patrick knew – and in his selfless way, he gave her his blessing and let her go.

Looking back across the years, Miranda could see how her reticence in the early days with Tony had served to stimulate his interest in her. He was a man so used to easy conquests that Miranda's cool reserve intrigued and increased his desire for her. He was constantly on the telephone, always sending her flowers, and continually monopolizing her free time.

She was working then for a women's magazine and had begun to take over the fashion side. In this capacity, she was sent over to Paris to cover the spring collections. When Tony heard about it, he said at once:

'I'm due for some leave. I'll come with you.'

'Don't be silly, Tony!' she laughed at him. 'I'll be busy the whole time at the shows or going out with buyers.'

He seemed to accept this but to her amused astonishment, when she took her place in the Viscount which was to fly her over to Orly Airport, she found Tony in the seat beside her.

'You must be mad!' she said, but she was intrigued, too. He must have gone to quite a bit of trouble to find her flight number and seat ticket and get on board like this. She hadn't even noticed him at the airport.

'Surprise, surprise! Here, I bought these for you to wear!'

He handed her a beautiful shoulder spray of white camellias.

'Must have you looking smart in front of all the Diors and what-have-you,' he chuckled.

She had to take the spray – touched and amused by such gallantry. Tony really was indefatigable.

But she was not quite so pleased when she discovered that he had also booked an adjoining room at her hotel in Paris.

'I'm not going to sleep with you, Tony,' she said bluntly as he came into her room, grinning disarmingly. The porter had just left the luggage and apparently at Tony's request unlocked the communicating door.

He put his arms round her and kissed her, feeling her stiffen as he did so.

'Tony, no!'

'Mandy, darling, why not? You're not really so very conventional, are you?'

'It isn't just a question of morals or conventions, Tony. It's just that I don't want an affair.'

She was equally determined that she would not get on to this sort of footing with him. She had never wanted a casual sexual relationship with any man. In order to be able to give her body, she must love the man to whom she was giving herself. Her brief affair with Alastair had taught her that there was no lasting happiness for a woman in promiscuous relationships. And although she found Tony amusing and attractive, she was not in love with him.

But Paris in the spring, the glow of ardent youth, the expectancy of romance, and Tony's increasing pursuit slowly undermined her.

He could be as crazy, as eager, as persistent as Patrick, and at the same time so much smoother, more subtle and more experienced.

'I'm madly in love with you – you know that, darling. Why must you go on being so remote, so cold? You're *not* really cold. I swear you're not.'

He was once more in her bedroom after she had dined with him. He had followed her into her room despite her firm goodnight in the corridor. She freed herself from a long and impassioned embrace.

'I'm not cold, Tony, but I've told you before, there is no long-term happiness for either of us in a causal love affair.'

He looked disappointed, boyish and appealing that night as he stood there staring dejectedly at her, re-arranging his tie.

'I think I know what's in your mind, Mandy. No sex without a wedding ring. Is that it?'

'I didn't say that. But there must be love. Sex for its own sake is not for me. I can't give myself to a man just because I find him physically attractive. It's tied up with all the important things of life, particularly love – real love.'

He said at once:

'But I do love you – I do, Mandy. I haven't looked at another woman since I met you. I'm absolutely crazy about you.'

He sounded completely sincere. Her heart softened. He was certainly a most attractive and likeable person. Several of the women journalists whom she knew and had met again at the shows would have given a great deal to be in her shoes with Tony constantly in attendance. When Tony came into a room, women always looked at him twice. He had immense sex appeal. Miranda knew that there were a great many of them who would possibly have slept with him if they had been asked.

Miranda was attracted, despite her dislike of the promiscuous. Tony was full of charm and so ardent that she felt instinctively he would be a desirable lover. But instinctively, too, she felt that he was not the kind of man to devote himself for a life-time to any one woman.

'It isn't fair to accuse me of womanizing, just because there have been many women in my past,' he defended himself. 'None of them meant what *you* mean to me, Mandy. You're the first woman I've ever known whom I feel I could settle down with. At least let me prove I can be faithful. Look – let's try it out for six months. If in that time you feel more sure about me, we can discuss marriage. I want *you* to be sure, too. Six months would decide for us both, wouldn't it? We can be very discreet – there's my flat and yours; Mandy, darling, *please*. Let me show how much I can love you. Give me a chance to make you love me.'

It was another month before she gave way. They'd both had a little too much to drink and were alone in Tony's flat – an attractively-decorated flat off St James Street, furnished with taste, full of good books and pictures and with a Bechstein piano. Tony played – improvised – and even sang in a light, charming baritone. They were lying on his bed. He caressed her, every moment becoming a little less controlled.

'You're so beautifully made for love,' he was saying. 'You torment me. It's damned unfair, darling. It isn't as if there's any real reason against our making love. You've said you find me attractive – I *know* you do. But at the last minute, you draw away. What's the matter with you? What are you afraid of?'

She knew that there was some justification in his accusations. She'd no right to allow him the intimacies of their constant embraces, only to call a halt at the last intimate step. It was no excuse to say whenever Tony became too ardent that she had spelt out to him her limits. In the end, she began to want him just as he wanted her and inevitably the night came when her will to resist him was at its lowest ebb. She suddenly drew him down to her and they made love quickly, violently. For both of them it was completely satisfying.

He refused to let her leave and she stayed the remainder of the night with him. He made love to her again – but this time with a slow, sensual delight until her physical surrender to him was absolute.

'I told you it would be perfect!' he whispered against her warm bare shoulder. 'I knew we were meant for each other, my darling!'

Lying with her arms round him, his dark head against her breast, she felt a dreamy languorous contentment new to her. In Tony's arms, she was all woman. Her emotions swung in heady excitement from tenderness to passionate desire; from a complete surrender to a primitive ecstasy of the senses and then to glorious fulfilment and release. Her mind and body seemed to overflow with a tenderness which came close to love – the sort of love she was seeking.

Tony raised himself on one elbow and reached across her to switch on the bedside lamp. It was not yet dawn. In the lamplight the small room looked strange to Miranda – unreal and unfamiliar. It was a man's room with dark, rich furniture, dark wine-coloured curtains, a tallboy, a wardrobe, a pile of luggage in one corner. A rather untidy array of his clothes and hers lay on the dark red carpet.

His arm rested lightly across her breasts. His touch gave her a quick, unexpected resurgence of excitement. He turned his head and looked down at her.

'You're beautiful, Mandy. More beautiful in love in the dawn than in your cool, pale, day-time loveliness. Your cheeks are flushed – your eyes are like great green sparkling pools of mystery. What are you thinking of, my darling?'

'Of you!' She smiled up at him, tracing the curve of his mouth. 'You do know how to make love to a woman!'

For an instant, the mouth looked almost sulky; the lower lip was full and bruised.

'You expected me to be inept?'

He was quick to suspect criticism, which he hated.

'No, darling. I'd be a fool if I did. I don't mind about the women in your past – only about your conquests in future.'

He smiled down at her, his hand lightly

tracing the curve between her breasts and sliding down past her small waist to her smooth thighs.

'Why should there be any women in my future? I have the most beautiful woman in the world to love. I don't need more conquests. God, Mandy, you were made for love! There must have been other men in your past. Tell me about them.'

'I don't want to think of or discuss anyone but you – us!'

Any curiosity he might have felt was swept aside as he felt her arms draw him down once again to the tantalizing temptation of her perfect body.

So the mad, breathless love-affair caught Miranda up and swept her on.

At first she refused to do as Tony wished and move into his flat. It wasn't just that she had no wish for their friends to know that they were sleeping together. She had never been conventional or afraid of her reputation. It was a reluctance to commit herself to a permanent affair. That worried her. While they lived apart, and Tony only came to her flat, or she to his, she could retain her independence between those frequent hours of impassioned desire. But with each period of time she spent with him, the longing increased to share more of her life with him and to become an intrinsic part of his. Tony was persistent.

'It's so damn silly, Mandy! Half your belongings are already in my flat, and I always seem to have left something behind in yours. Besides, darling, it's absolutely maddening if I suddenly feel a violent urge to make love to you and then have to get in a taxi and drive to your place or ring you up and tell you to come to mine. I want to be able to turn round and kiss you, then and there.'

A lot of what he said was true. She was forever leaving a lipstick or an earring or a pair of shoes at Tony's flat when, having overslept, she dashed off to the office. Tony often forgot his razor and had to go back to his own flat unshaved, which he hated. He was very fastidious. It was not a practical solution and it didn't achieve much towards that feeling of independence, because whenever she was apart from him she found herself wishing desperately that they were together.

A month after the affair had begun, she moved most of her clothes into his flat. Tony was delighted. He filled the rooms with flowers to welcome her. He made love to her before he allowed her to unpack, and again after she had finished – until she lay relaxed and laughing on his big double bed.

Her interest in her job all but ceased. She went to the office only because she felt she must stay financially independent of Tony no matter how she counted on him in the emotional sense. She insisted upon paying half the housekeeping; she contributed part of the rent. No amount of protests from Tony made her alter her mind.

Only one thing spoiled her growing contentment – Tony's absence practically every weekend.

'I just *have* to go, sweetheart! One day the old estates in Leicestershire will belong to me and my papa has made it quite clear that unless I take what he calls an *active* interest in the place, he'll leave the lot to my cousin Robin. In a way, one can see the old boy's point of view.'

She at once offered to accompany him but he had explained that his mother had had a stroke and was obliged to lead as quiet a life as possible.

'As a consequence, my father has forbidden visitors of any kind,' he'd said. 'Anyway, darling, even if I could take you, you'd be terribly bored. If you don't hunt like my father does, there's nothing whatever to do up there. The house is like a morgue. I'd never go near the place if duty to my parents did not oblige me to. Mother looks forward to seeing me.'

Though disappointed, she nevertheless understood and made a mental resolution never to ask Tony to stay in town during the weekend. Once or twice she was rewarded when he would turn to her on a Friday night and say:

'Hell, I just refuse to leave you this weekend. I'll ring up and say I've got to do some special work for the F.O.'

Then Saturday and Sunday became precious, unexpected gifts which she treasured and thought about through other weekends, which she spent mooning round the flat alone, longing for Monday and Tony's return. She avoided her old friends. She wanted to go nowhere – do nothing without Tony. He had grown necessary – far too much so – to her happiness. She felt only half alive when she was apart from him.

Gradually, his flat began to seem like her home as well as his, with her books and a few favourite ornaments or pictures around among his. It was like a marriage and she gave herself completely to the task of making life easy and beautiful and happy for Tony. They went out less and she began to cook – something she had always enjoyed and which brought back strange nostalgic memories of her early days as David's wife.

At first, Tony was amused by this unexpected domesticity.

'Quite the little housewife,' he teased.

But a few weeks later when he came home to find her dishing up a Spaghetti Bolognese, he said:

'Oh, are we dining in again?'

Something in his tone made her look up at him sharply.

'Did you want to go out? I'm afraid it's just about ready.'

He flung his coat and umbrella on to the kitchen chair and went through to the sitting-room to pour out a drink.

'It doesn't matter,' he said vaguely.

She left the spaghetti boiling in the saucepan and went through to join him.

'Sure?'

'Of course I'm sure. What's got into you, Mandy?'

He handed her a glass of sherry and picked up the evening paper which lay beside his briefcase.

She watched him silently and then said:

'You haven't kissed me!'

He glanced up at her and held out a hand.

'Come and sit down, sweet. I'll remedy the situation.'

But she stayed standing. A sudden tiny chill of apprehension stole over her.

He gave her a brief, cool smile.

'Okay, if you want to sulk.'

'Tony!' The reproach in her voice was also a plea.

He picked up the paper although he did not read it.

'Mandy, what *is* the matter? I've had a pretty grim day at the office. Must I come back to find you in a mood? What the hell's wrong?'

Later, as she lay in his arms, her eyes full of

tears, she tried to remember what the original 'mood' – as he called it – had been about. She wondered if Tony was right and if it had all been her fault. It was she who had been the one to put an end to misunderstanding – to throw pride on one side, and say:

'Darling, don't let's fight, please. I can't *bear* it.'

And she had run across the room and flung herself into his arms, feeling almost as if she had been reprieved when he ruffled her hair and said:

'Okay, sweet. Let's make it up – in bed!'

Their love-making had been quick and sure, and as satisfying as always. Only when it was over was she aware once again of a difference in him. It was as if they had entered a new phase in their relationship. Tony got up from the bed almost at once and said cheerfully:

'Come on, darling. Time we had that meal – or will it be ruined? I know, let's go out and get something to eat at Prunier's, then go on to Geoff's party.'

'Geoff?'

'Yes – he's one of my colleagues at work. He's giving a drinks party and told me to bring you along. It won't really get going much before ten so we've plenty of time.'

She dressed slowly and reluctantly. She had had quite a heavy day at the office and what with that and the emotional upset, followed by their love-making, she was not in the mood for a late night party. It was obvious now that Tony had wanted to go right from the start. Maybe the domestic routine of the meals at home was beginning to bore him *Could it be she was beginning to bore him, too?*

However, she forgot her misapprehensions as she joined Tony in the sitting-room. He gave one look at her and whistled.

'Mmm! That black is really something, darling. I haven't seen you in it before, have I? Come over here and be kissed.'

'You'll spoil my make-up, Tony!'

'Hell to that!' he said and kissed her. 'For two pins, I'd scrap Geoff's party and put you back to bed. On the other hand, I can't resist the thought of showing you off. Geoff has been dying of curiosity for weeks now.'

They went to Geoffrey's flat in Baker Street.

She hadn't liked him and she hadn't liked the way all the guests got drunk. Tony, too, had far too much liquor. It was only because she realized he was tight that she found it possible to ignore the fact that he flirted quite shamelessly with a dark, rather voluptuous brunette who, she was told, was one of the new secretaries in Tony's department.

It was three in the morning before she got Tony home and helped him to undress and get into bed. Too exhausted to sleep, she took two aspirins and then overslept in the morning. Rushing to dress and to get to the office on time, she had no time in which to brood over Tony's behaviour.

But during subsequent weeks, she had several occasions in which to think about it. Tony's manner towards her was growing far more casual. There was a subtle, gradual change in him. The more devotion she lavished upon him, the more he seemed to take it – and her – for granted. She began to feel miserably unhappy. She realized that she had been handling Tony the wrong way. While she was reserved and aloof, his interest in her had been keen and constant. The moment she let herself go and allowed him to see that she adored him, he had become at first indifferent – then bored. She knew that the present relationship couldn't continue. She grew nervy and irritable and lost weight. She chided herself for having allowed herself to get caught up in a love affair like this. It was just what she had dreaded. She had drifted into it simply through lack of self-control – pandering to the urgent call of her body and kidding herself that it was love he had offered her.

One night, gathering her pride as a successful antidote to the weakness of this still powerful, physical longing for Tony, she told him that she was leaving him.

He looked at her in amazement.

'*Leaving* me! But why? Darling, you can't really mean it. What's wrong? What have I done?'

'Nothing! It's just that – well, I'm not happy and I feel it's best to put an end to our life together.'

There was nothing casual about Tony now. He was full of concern. He pleaded with her to stay with him. He tried every argument. Bitterly she saw that her very announcement that she meant to leave him had re-awakened his old desire.

'I love you, Mandy. You *can't* go. There must be more to it than you've told me. Have you met someone else?'

'No! I love you, Tony. Don't look so surprised. It's because I love you that I'm leaving you.'

He frowned uneasily.

'You mean you want me to ask you to marry me?'

'You're not the marrying kind, Tony. You've often said so. You don't want to be tied down.'

He drew a deep breath, and taking hold of her hand began to play reflectively with her fingers.

'It isn't quite that, darling. You don't really know me very well, do you? Perhaps it's my fault for not having been entirely honest with you. But I couldn't be, Mandy – you see, I was so afraid of losing you.'

He gave a quick look at her curious face and then turned away.

'I – I know I should have told you, but … well, the truth is, I *can't* marry you. You see, I'm married already.'

'You're *what?*' She was so astounded she could think of nothing else to say.

'I know it must be a shock. I lied when I said I had to go home weekends to see the estate. The fact is, I went to see my wife. Don't look like that, Mandy, you don't understand. She's the one who had the stroke, not Mother. Of course, I could get a divorce but – well, it has always seemed to me that to do so would be like kicking a fellow when he's down. Do you understand? You see now why I haven't been able to offer you anything more than this…' he swept his hand round the flat vaguely. 'You *know* I love you, Mandy. If I were free to marry, we'd have married ages ago. You do believe that, don't you?'

She had believed him because it never once occurred to her that anyone could lie about such a thing. It certainly explained those weekends which despite the explanation he had given at the time about helping his father, had somehow not rung quite true. Had she known he was married, she would never have moved in with him. He had lied in order to get what he wanted. It was dishonest and cruel. In a way, she did not find it easy to forgive. But on the other hand, she felt a deep stirring of pity for him, and a strange, contrary admiration because he stood by the woman he had married even though she could never be a real wife to him again.

Tony held her hand and gave her a few brief details as to how his wife had shown symptoms during their honeymoon – how she had grown worse as the weeks went by and finally had the stroke. It was tragic – even before their first year of marriage ended.

'Please don't leave me, Mandy. You may think I managed my life quite satisfactorily without you before we met but now it's all different – I couldn't be happy without you. I need you desperately.'

She needed him, too. She had settled down in what now seemed like her home and had grown accustomed to Tony's place in her life; perhaps more than anything else, she had developed this ceaseless need for their sexual relationship. They were completely united as lovers, and even although familiarity had in some way slightly lessened Tony's desire, it had in fact increased her own pleasure in being his lover.

'I must think it over!' she told him, knowing that she needed more time to adjust herself to his incredible news.

That night, Tony was as ardent as he had been the first time they made love. She clung to him, trying to convince herself that she didn't really love him. It was just sex and the fear of living alone again which made her want so desperately to stay with him.

Her heart remained uneasy as the weeks went by until she was forced finally to see Tony for what he really was – a weak, self-indulgent boy who wouldn't grow up. First there were a few evenings when he had been 'late at the office' – Tony, who never put in a moment's extra work if he could help it. Finally, another party at Geoff's but one to which this time *she* was not invited.

'You do understand, don't you, darling? It's really just for people in the office.'

He came home with lipstick on his face and shirt.

'For God's sake, Mandy, you're behaving like a jealous wife. It was only a harmless bit of fun.'

And then came the phone call the next morning and a feminine, youthful voice asking if this were Tony Barrance's number. Some sixth sense made Miranda inform the caller she was his housekeeper.

There was a pause and a giggle and then a girlish voice said:

'When Mr Barrance comes in, will you tell him he left his umbrella in my flat last night. Tell him he's welcome to come and get it any time.'

First he tried to pretend there'd been nothing in it; then made light of what he called 'a harmless bit of fun'.

'That's the second time you've used the phrase, Tony. I realize I have no right to insist that you be faithful to me and I no longer care whether you are or not.'

He shrugged his shoulders.

'Damn it all, Mandy, there's no need to hit the roof. I give you my word it didn't mean a thing.'

His handsome face looked sulky.

'I reckon I've been pretty faithful, considering.'

'Considering we aren't married?'

She turned away from him, walked into her bedroom and began to pack her belongings. Tony tried pleading, then sulked and finally attempted to make love to her. She tore his hands away and stared at him, white-faced.

'Don't touch me. It's all over. Tony – that's final. Now let me go.'

As time went by, she had grown to think of him more calmly, and with less revulsion. She blamed herself rather than him for she realized that he was incapable of behaving in a different fashion. She even felt relieved that the existence of his poor wife had made it impossible for them to be married. She tried to remember the good times they had

had together.

She did not see him again.

She looked at him now in the Cappello at Siena, all these years later, and despite herself, felt the old stirring of attraction. For an instant, the look in his eyes sparked off an answer in her own – then it was gone. No, never again, she thought grimly.

'You're looking well, Tony,' she said and gently removed her hand from beneath his. 'Now, if you'll excuse me, I must go.'

She felt herself smiling at the hurt surprise in Tony's eyes as she stood up and walked away from him. She knew that she would have some explaining to do to Peter and Sue but she didn't mind. One thing she had no wish to do was to get caught up with Tony again.

Sue had not appeared in the bar during her brief encounter with Tony, so she went in search of her.

There was only one woman in the cloak-room – no sign of Sue there. Puzzled, Miranda asked the woman if she had seen a fair girl in a green suit. The woman powdering her face, nodded. Yes, she had left a moment ago.

'It's terribly hot in that bar,' the woman said as Miranda stood beside her and checked her make up. 'I've just been looking for my husband. I couldn't see him so I came in here to escape those ogling Italian men. Tony may not have arrived yet as I am rather early. We said eight o'clock.'

Sheer curiosity forced the words from Miranda's lips.

'I've just been talking to a man in the bar called Tony Barrance. I wonder...'

'I'm Enid Barrance!' the other said, slightly puzzled by the swift rush of colour that flamed now across Miranda's face.

'So you know my husband?'

'We used to know each other a long time ago,' Miranda said awkwardly. 'It was quite a surprise seeing him in the bar after all these years. He didn't tell me that he'd married again.'

'Again? No, my dear, I'm the only wife Tony ever had.'

Miranda bit her lip. So the desperately-ill wife had recovered after all. What an amazing way life had of twisting things.

'I rather think that you may have been the victim of one of Tony's fantastic stories,' Mrs Barrance said, gently. 'What was it this time? Was I supposed to be a helpless invalid? In a mental home? Or at death's door?' Her face twisted into an amused smile. 'He'll really have to think of something else for his next conquest!'

Seeing Miranda's hot flushed face, she put her hand on her arm and said:

'I'm afraid I've shocked you. I only hope

you weren't hurt.'

'I was thinking of you,' Miranda said. 'How awful it must have been for you.'

'No! Many years ago I learned to accept my husband for what he is. I suppose you'd call him a rotter – to use an old-fashioned but appropriate word. But in his own peculiar way he loves me. The others come and go but he always comes back to me. So you see, it is "the others" who get hurt, for they expect something from him he's quite unable to give.'

'And you can be happy like that?' Miranda asked incredulously.

'I daresay I'm as happy as any of us are in this world,' sighed Tony's wife. 'After all, happiness is a very transient thing, isn't it? Maybe the bitterness and frustration and loneliness that one so often feels give women like me the power to appreciate more fully the perfect moments.'

She has come to terms with life, Miranda thought enviously, liking and admiring her and at the same time knowing she would never be able to think kindly of Tony again.

'It doesn't seem fair that Tony should always get away with it,' she said as they stood up to go.

Her companion smiled.

'Oh, he doesn't get off scot-free. This trip to Siena is part of his penance for the last affair. He can't stand sight-seeing and I've always longed to see this city. Tomorrow we go back to Rome and he can have his night clubs again. This way, we both get what we want out of our marriage.'

Miranda laughed and felt a great lifting of her spirits. Nobody, she thought wryly, was better fitted than Enid Barrance to be Tony's wife – and nobody she had ever met had seemed quite so sane.

CHAPTER EIGHT

Miranda listened to the sound of David's footsteps in the kitchenette adjoining the studio and tried to steady the trembling of her hands and the hurried beating of her heart. It was absurd to let herself become so overwrought, so tensed. David had seemed completely at ease, delighted to see her but quite controlled.

She looked around her. It was obvious that a lot of water had rolled under the financial bridge for David. Of course she knew that he had done well. The first year after she had left him she had seen a notice in one of the papers of an exhibition he had given, and the critics had praised his work highly. Soon after she married John she had also read another notice about a portrait David had painted of a famous duchess. She had thought then: *'David was always good at portraits.* He *is* getting on!'

But that was all that she had known. Now she found herself in his studio. Great crimson velvet curtains framed the enormous windows from which she could see across the roof-tops. Several paintings – landscapes as well as portraits – were hung on the walls.

There were piles of canvases, some finished, some virgin, leaning against each other. On an old oak side-table of Dutch design he kept fruit and drinks. It moved her to remember how David had always loved fruit – sometimes refused to eat anything else all day when he was painting. At one end of the studio stood a big divan covered with a crimson and gold-brocaded spread. There was some central heating but the ceiling was so high that it was quite cold in here.

David came back into the room and placed an ice bucket on a tray with some bottles. He put it down on the table beside her.

'Quite fantastic running into you in the Underground after all these years!' he said, as he came towards her, his blue eyes smiling their pleasure in their unexpected reunion.

'Gin and tonic!' he announced and then with a familiar upward sweep of dark brows... 'You do still prefer it to brandy or whisky? I should have asked...'

'No, this will be fine!' Miranda broke in, glad that her voice at least was steady.

David gave her the drink, then sat down on a wooden stool opposite her. He raised his glass.

'To old times, Mandy. I must say, when we first ran into each other I simply couldn't believe it was you. Not that you've changed much – but, oh, well, I suppose you were the last person in the world I expected to see in the Tube. I suppose I've always imagined you in the Caribbean or Paris; somewhere really chic!'

He hasn't changed much either, Miranda thought, listening to the boyish voice.

The boy had, of course, become a man but the years had served him kindly and added to his attraction. The lines around eyes and mouth gave his face character, and a look of strength which was pleasantly masculine. As a young man he had been almost too good looking.

'Now tell me, what were you doing? Where were you going? I want to know all about you.'

Miranda's gaze went swiftly down to her drink. She wouldn't tell him she had been on her way to the studio for the third time in the vague hope of finding him there. She had learned something from life – not to be too honest; with Tony, anyway, it didn't pay.

'I was going to visit a friend!'

He accepted her explanation and said with enthusiasm:

'Well, I'm damned glad I caught that particular train at the right moment to divert you. You'll stay and have supper with me, won't you? Or do you have to rush home?'

'I don't have to go anywhere!' she said quickly. 'You may as well know … John and

I have separated for the time being and I'm quite free to come and go as I please. I'd like to have some supper with you. I want to hear all about your work. Do you know I met Ludwig Strupner a few weeks ago when I was in Paris? He asked after you.'

'Good heavens! Ludwig Strupner! I've seen his work mentioned from time to time in the papers. Haven't actually come across him, though, since … since our wedding…'

David's voice trailed off. He gave a swift, searching look at Miranda's face. She looked pale but very beautiful, he thought. She wore the sort of clothes he admired – plain, well-cut, exquisite; and her gloves and shoes and bag were expensive – impeccable. Elegant, lovely Miranda.

'That was a long while ago, Mandy. I … oh, I suppose it's silly for us to pretend there isn't a past, and yet somehow I don't find it easy to talk about *us*.'

She felt her heart give a quick leap of pleasure. So he wasn't indifferent.

'You're very quiet. Do you smoke? Have one of these. Let me get you another drink…' He handed her a box of cigarettes and suddenly grinned. 'Do you know, I feel quite shy with you, Mandy. I didn't think it was possible for me to be shy with a woman after all this time. I wonder why…' He gave her a long, searching look.

'You know, you are far more beautiful now

than you ever were as a young girl,' he added. 'I'd like to paint you. Would you sit for me?'

Was it the artist in him or the man who was appreciating her? She wasn't sure. It didn't even matter very much. As she sat listening to him, watching him, learning to know him all over again, she felt that she was well on thc way once more to being snared in the trap – as surely as she had been the day they first met. She loved him. Perhaps she had always loved him.

'Mandy, I don't believe you're listening to one word I say. You're miles away. You're not sorry we ran into each other, that we've met again? You're not still cross about the past?'

'Cross?' The word jumped from her lips in astonishment. 'What an odd word.'

'I wouldn't blame you if you were. I know I behaved very badly. I was appallingly selfish, a complete egoist. Perhaps all artists are the same. I was taken up with my work, bent on proving myself to be a good painter. I neglected you and I know it. After you divorced me, I was well aware I'd been a damned fool – worst of all was the knowledge that I had only myself to blame.'

Miranda was staggered. Remembering the years with him – and the end – she saw the breakup of their marriage as something that had been beyond the help of either of them. Force of circumstances, a series of misunderstandings and failures on both sides, had undermined their urgent youthful passion and finally destroyed their love.

She clasped and unclasped her long fingers nervously.

'You – you never tried to get in touch with me after I left.'

David got up and walked over to the large window. It occupied almost the entire wall. The sky was turning a smoky blue in the spring twilight. The studio was ideal for a painter. The view was magnificent.

'Perhaps it was partly pride – but I didn't think you would ever forgive me. You said we'd come to the end and I suppose I thought you must be right. We certainly couldn't have gone on as we were.'

'We were both failures!' Miranda said quietly. 'We failed each other.'

David swung round and stared at her across the darkening room.

'Yet I loved you, Mandy. I fell in love with you the first time I ever saw you. And what I felt that day went deeper, and is bigger than anything that happened to me since you left. I've looked for you in all the other women since then; perhaps succeeded in finding a part of you here, and another part there – a bit in another girl's smile, or voice. But these affairs never lasted with me, for sooner or later I was forced to recognize that the girl just wasn't *you*. I've often wondered if I'd ever be given the chance to tell you this. Well – now you know and I won't blame you for doubting the truth of it.'

Miranda remained perfectly still, afraid to move lest the slightest noise should shatter the dreamlike quality of the moment. Her unexpected meeting with David – the way he had led her, unresisting, to the studio, and now this strange revelation of his feelings – all seemed as unreal as a fantasy; a dream which might suddenly vanish and leave her floundering once more in her hopeless search for the love which was truth – the truth which was the quintessence of life.

A tiny warning bell rang at the back of her mind. David had always found words easy. Sometimes he would be carried away by his own command of language and the truth could become confused with a fictitious unreality. She used to call it his way of painting verbal pictures. In the early days of their marriage she had told him that his paintings were more honest than he was, emotionally.

Did he know now what he was saying? She could barely see his face through the shadows. But she could feel the excitement, the increasing tension between them.

'Haven't you found happiness, David?' she asked.

He came back across the room and stood behind her chair. She felt his fingers touch the top of her head and move gently down the shining gold of her hair until they rested on the nape of her neck. He used to admire her neck and never tired of sketching it.

'How can I possibly answer that question?' he said at last. 'Happiness can come from so many things. I'm happy when I know I've painted a good picture. I'm happy when the phone rings and I find I've got a new, important client – a commission to paint a portrait. It's always good to know I have been chosen in preference to a dozen other portrait-painters in this country. I'm happy when I can hear Maria Callas sing – or Menuhin play, watch Fonteyn dance; when I see the first daffodils bursting into bloom – the dew on the grass – the view from this window. But these are mere moments when life seems rich and good and well worth the ugliness, bitterness and the disappointments. But happiness is so transient. *We* found it once, didn't we, Mandy? Yet we let it float away from us like a bubble, and burst in our very sight!'

She was on her feet now. For the first time she was moved to speak.

'David, dear, *dear* David – we were so young. We didn't appreciate the value of what we had. *I* have never found it again, either.'

They were facing each other now in the darkness.

'Is that why you've separated from your husband?'

She lifted her shoulders with a vague gesture of uncertainty.

'I don't really know. I used to think life was so simple and that I knew most of the answers. As I've grown older I seem to have become less and less certain about the reason for anything – either good or bad.'

'You've certainly grown up, Mandy.'

'But there must be an answer to it all, David. It can't be right just to wander through life taking each day as it comes without real understanding; without purpose; not caring much about past or future – living only in the present. I suddenly realized that *I* was living in a dangerous vacuum. I knew I didn't want to go on with what seemed only half a life. I wanted entirety. There was no particular unhappiness for me but no real happiness, either. At least in *our* marriage, David, I was wholly alive. I felt both joy and pain in the extreme. *But I felt it.* Perhaps that's why I was the wrong wife for you. An artist needs someone quiet and peaceful and rather domesticated, who can fade into the background of his life and come forward only when he needs her. I suppose I was too demanding, too insecure; jealous of your work, too. I was horribly possessive. Because you were all of my life, I expected to be all of yours. But you had the ability to divorce yourself completely from the soul-destroying, domestic trivialities that surrounded us; the unpaid bills, the desperate efforts to make ends meet. The daily routine of marriage bored and irritated you. If I'd been older and more experienced, I'd have known how to protect you from that side of our life together. As it was, I resented your unwillingness to share the difficulties as well as the pleasures "of love on a shoe-string". I wasn't ready to be made a burnt offering on the altar of an artist's ambition.'

He walked away from her, lit a candle in a silver sconce on the side table, and in that soft light poured out two more drinks for Miranda and himself.

'I wouldn't have wanted you to be different. Don't you understand that I loved you not only for your beauty, but for each one of those facets of your character which you are deploring and which make up the whole? If you'd been a dull, domesticated creature who could have coped in the kitchen and left me alone, I would never have fallen in love with you in the first place. I adored *you* as you were – so full of vitality and gaiety and feeling. You plunged into life with a passionate intensity that equalled my own. You were as gloriously crazy as I was. You could be gentle, too, and adorably loving. You had no false pride, no inhibitions. When you gave yourself to me, it was with your whole heart. It is I who should have been different, more tolerant and understanding of you as a wife as well as a mistress. You didn't fail me, Mandy. I failed you. I never imagined you would forgive me for what I did to you and even if I never see you again after this day, I shall be grateful for this meeting – for being able to admit the truth about *us*.'

She felt an overwhelming sense of futility – tinged with despair. This was a new David, capable of intelligent self-analysis, and an altogether unsuspected sympathy with her side of the matter. If he had only been like this when their marriage first began to go wrong, she would never have left him, never have felt the warm sweet love within her twist and turn into something like cold dislike. It seemed easy now to forgive him, but what good could it do? He had made a new life for himself – a life without her. They could never capture the past or bridge the gulf of the corroding years.

As if sensing her sudden despair, he spoke more lightly.

'We're getting ourselves depressed with all this talk of the past. We're supposed to be having a celebration drink – remember? Drink up, Mandy, then I'd like to take you to my favourite little restaurant. It's only a couple of minutes' walk from here and I think it would amuse you. It's down in a basement – nothing glamorous – but the right atmosphere. Candlelight, which you know I like. The food's Continental and extremely good, and the place is always full of entertaining artistic celebrities.'

He had once again become the enthusiastic, impulsive, companion that she remembered so well. Slowly she began to respond to his lightheartedness. She powdered her nose, combed her hair and found herself laughing with him as they walked arm in arm down the quiet back streets to David's favourite haunt. The emotional tension of their sudden unexpected meeting had gone. Yet she was still aware of the clasp of his hand holding hers and felt that she was vibrating and warm and truly alive again. She refused to think of tomorrow or the next day. It was good enough to be with him and find herself able to joke and reminisce and be able to turn her head and look at his familiar face, and say to herself: *This is my David. He is real. He is no longer just a memory.*

In the restaurant – candlelit as he had promised and full of delectable odours – surrounded by clever murals on white-washed walls, they sat at a corner table and David ordered a wine they both used to like. She studied him and tried to decide why his face was so attractive to her.

His hair was a light brown, curling a little

on the top. He had curiously high cheek bones, and the narrow, observant eyes of a painter. It was not a remarkable face, but interesting, and strong. He had neither Tony's dark Latin fascination nor Patrick's primitive appeal; he was not tall and debonair and distinguished like Ludwig, who in his younger days had been so attractive. He had none of Harry's freckled, youthful appeal. David might have passed unnoticed in a crowd of other men of his age, yet for her, his face – like the man himself – was special. He fascinated her.

He introduced her to a friend who came over to their table for a drink; a well-known author who paid Miranda a number of extravagant compliments. She felt childishly glad that David seemed jealous because the man kept looking at her – and sulked until he left them alone once more. Clearly David didn't want to share her with anyone.

They did not wait for coffee.

'We might just as well have it in peace at home. This place is too full tonight.' he grinned at her as they walked back to the penthouse, arm in arm.

The large studio room seemed chilly after the crowded little restaurant. David saw Miranda shiver and at once switched on an electric fire which sent a warm, golden glow into the room. While he was in the kitchenette making coffee, she curled up on the divan and leant back against the pile of cushions, relaxed and strangely happy. It pleased her that David could still be jealous when another man looked at her with desire. She appreciated his new maturity, but nevertheless was glad to find in him traces of the younger David who had been so completely hers for a while.

When he came back with the coffee tray, she smiled at him.

'It was a lovely dinner, David. I liked the restaurant – and your friend, the novelist, too. He wrote *"Beware"*, didn't he? A brilliant book. He was most amusing.'

David gave her a quick look then his lips curved into a smile.

'All right, so I was jealous! I didn't like the way he monopolized you, though I can't say I blame him. You know, Mandy, your modesty has always surprised me. Don't you realize what you do to men, with that shining golden beauty of yours? Tonight you look like a cool clear stream – perhaps you know the kind I mean. It may seem calm as it flows by, but underneath the surface there lies a turbulence, a violence that can be as exciting to a man as a whirlpool. You sit there looking like the Mona Lisa, half-smiling at me from those, incredible eyes of yours, and I haven't the faintest idea what you're really thinking or feeling. Tell me, Mandy. Tell me your thoughts.'

He had re-lit his beloved candles. They cast flickering shadows on his paintings – on the high ceiling, and on her face. He looked at her intently.

The smile left her lips as she stared back at him. The coffee grew cold in the little porcelain cup she held in one hand.

'I'm not sure you would really be glad to know my thoughts.'

He took her cup away and sat down on the long low divan beside her, taking both her hands in his.

'I would, Mandy. Bad or good, I want them. Don't you realize what meeting you again means to me? For years I've imagined how I'd feel if I ran into you. Often I've been tempted to try and find you, but I honestly believed you were happily married. Every once in a while I've read bits about you in the newspapers – you seemed fully occupied. I imagined you'd found your niche – and your man – and forgotten all about me. Or if not quite that, I presumed I was merely an unpleasant memory. If that is all I do mean to you, I'd like to know now before I become any deeper involved. Reason tells me that I can't mean anything much to you, yet something here–' he put his hand over his heart – 'my instinct, if you like, tells me that you're not all that indifferent. For God's sake, Mandy, don't keep me in suspense. Tell me how you truly feel now we've met up again.'

Their thoughts had travelled on parallel lines. Reason did not allow that a love that was supposed to be dead could ever be revived. Hadn't somebody once written the word: *'Nothing is so dead as a dead love'?* Yet it had become clear to her this evening that she still loved David and that she still meant something to him.

'I love you David. I don't think I ever stopped loving you.'

As she spoke, she heard him draw in his breath sharply. A moment later, his arms were round her and his lips were against hers, fiercely demandingly.

She leaned back against the cushions and lay with her eyes closed, every nerve alive as his body embraced her own. As the pressure of his kiss lessened, she began to kiss him back. Her arms went round him and pulled him back to her.

'Mandy, Mandy!' His voice was a murmur against her mouth. Then she felt his lips against her throat and his hands began to search for the pearl buttons on her blouse.

'Let me!' she whispered, knowing his fingers would never be able to cope with the tiny button-holes. She longed for him to touch her – knew herself lost in this surge of passion. As he undressed her slowly, skilfully and all the time adoringly, the past became confused with the present. She relived their honeymoon, those first glorious days and nights of discovering each other. Then, too, David had undressed her, caressed her as his hands were now caressing her warm, vibrant body. Then, as now, she responded to his touch until she wanted him, wanted him with a blinding urgency that could not be denied.

'I love you – I *love* you!'

They were the last words she heard from him before her eyes closed and she surrendered herself completely to him.

Past and present were fused as though there had been no gap – no other men – no other loves – only David.

CHAPTER NINE

David took her quickly, his fierce passion drawing from her a quick and perfect response. They were completely in tune – moving to the same familiar beat of shared physical delight. They loved without reservation, with complete, mutual understanding. Finally she lay with eyes closed, her cheek against his chest, hearing and feeling the quietening of his heart's pounding. Her thoughts came quickly in brilliant flashes, each on a revelation.

I still love him. He still loves me – he still needs me. It has all begun again. It's happened so quickly, and so perfectly. David, my darling. David!...

'Mandy, my sweetheart!' That was a name from the past. She used always to be his sweetheart. Gently, he raised his head and kissed her lips. She kissed him back and smiled up at him. The firelight flickered over his face, transforming it for her.

'You're not cold? I'm not too heavy?' he asked her.

'No, no, *no!*' She pulled him down to her again. His weight was gloriously exhilarating to her. Her whole body ached with love for him and she was not willing for him to leave her yet.

'I'm all yours, Mandy, absolutely yours. You believe me, don't you?'

'M'mm!' Her eyes stared up at him with a mixture of faith and the old torment of cynical disbelief.

'It isn't just sex. That has a lot to do with it of course, but it isn't all.'

'I know!' she capitulated, kissing him tenderly, lovingly.

'You're my woman,' he said, 'the only woman I've ever really loved. No one but you has been able to make me feel like this. Just looking at you, watching you tonight, was enough to drive me mad. The touch of your hand, your Mona Lisa smile, your voice – they excite me in a way I can't possibly explain. I've met a lot of exciting women, Mandy, but with you it is always different – it's a miracle. Do you know what I mean?'

She nodded. Her mind, her heart, warmed to his words as, a moment ago, her body had leaped and responded to his passion. For her, too, it had never been the same with any other man. With Ludwig, she had felt perhaps a similar degree of sexual excitement and pleasure, but never had there been the same spiritual joy a woman received from perfect unity with the man she really loves.

'You're my man, David – and I'm your woman!'

It was as simple, as basic, as that!

'Remember our honeymoon, Mandy? Our first time? It was barely over before I wanted you again.'

She smiled.

'And each time was more exciting than the last. Tonight it has been the best of all.'

'Because we once lost each other, we've learned to put a greater value on our love.'

He stroked her hair.

'If you'd disappeared without letting me make love to you, I'd have gone crazy. All evening, I knew I had to have you, yet I didn't dare to hope... Mandy, darling, darling, *darling* – I still can't quite believe you're with me again, so close, so beautiful.'

'As close as we can be!' she whispered. 'I wish we could stay like this for ever and ever and ever–'

'Suicide pact?'

'No!' she smiled. 'It's far too lovely a feeling for me to want to put an end to it. I just wish time could stand still.'

'You'd get cold, cramped...'

'You'd get hungry!'

'Only for you.'

But at last with a sigh he drew away from her and lay propped on one elbow so that he could go on looking at her. Very gently he traced the outline of her cheek, no longer pale but flushed with the pink glow of love-making. His fingers moved to her creamy-white shoulders and down the long graceful lines of her body to the perfection of the small waist, curving hips and long tapering legs.

'How beautiful you are, Mandy. The years haven't altered that classic figure. Your loveliness makes me catch my breath. You are almost unbearably desirable. Yours is that strange fascination which can draw a man back to you again and again; make him feel he will never be satiated. I've never known this same desire for any other woman. Obviously, it was because I didn't love them as I love you.'

Miranda caught his hand and put it to her cheek.

'Tell me, David – what *is* love? What do *you* mean by love?'

He shrugged his shoulders, smoothed back his hair.

'Like you, I used to think I knew the answer to that. But I don't. I'm only sure of one thing – now that I've found you again, I can't let you go. You'll stay with me, won't you? I can't live without you. I need you physically, mentally, and above all, as an inspiration. Even now I can feel the burning need to paint you just as you look at this moment, your eyes as pure blue as aqua-marines. Your very smile is a challenge. I'd give a lot to catch that expression of softness and sadness; as though you are quite happy and yet can't believe it will last.'

'*Can* it last?'

Her hands clutched at his arms as if only physical contact could give her reassurance.

'You must be completely honest with me, David,' she went on. 'No more playing games, darling. No more dissembling. *I don't want an affair with you.* There have been too many with others and they were all the outcome of a desperate search for you, the need to be with you again. Where you are concerned I have no pride. I don't think I could bear it if anything went wrong between us a second time and I lost you all over again. Do you understand? If we begin again, it must be because we both believe it's for ever.'

'Yes, that's the way I want it, too. We should never have parted in the first place, Mandy. I don't want anything in the world but you – you and my work. You know what painting means to me. I couldn't give that up. It is an integral part of my life. But then you wouldn't want me to give it up, would you?'

She shook her head. She'd always known that David was first and foremost an artist and secondly her lover. But she would never be jealous of the artist again. She had learned her lesson. She was alive again for the first time in sixteen years. She couldn't tell him yet that already in the recess of her mind she was thinking of another Melanie, another child to replace the baby they had lost. Curiously enough, she had never since then wanted children.

She wondered how David would feel about her having a child, but it was too soon to speak of it. For the present they would have time only for each other. She must get to know him all over again, learn to live with him, share his work, his friends, his life.

'Where do you live, David?' she asked dreamily. 'Here in the studio?'

'Much of the time, yes. But I'm away quite a bit. I've just returned from a trip to America. I also have a small Georgian house in Gerrards Cross. The old days of financial hardship are over, Mandy. I wonder how different things might have been if we'd had more money when we first started?'

'Don't,' she whispered. 'Don't lets talk of money or the past, David. Let's think only of now – and our future.'

'Well, my darling, you said your time was your own. In that case you won't have to hurry away, will you? You'll stay here, in the studio, with me.'

She had no wish to return to her hotel in Sloane Street where she had been staying since her return from Italy. The unfriendly, impersonal hotel bedroom would be intolerable. She could not bear to leave this love – this warm, beautiful loving.

'I'll have to go back tomorrow and collect some clothes – if you want me to move in with you permanently.'

'*If* I want it!' He laughed. His face, she thought, was as young and as happy as the face of the David she had first known. He caught her in his arms and kissed her wildly. 'Life is going to be wonderful for us, darling. We can stay here together as long as we wish, cut off from the rest of the world. Only my daily, Mrs Dyer, comes to clean the studio. My friends are forbidden to bother me here unless they are invited. Mrs Dyer is the soul of discretion. I may have to go away for a week or so in the early summer. I've just met what you might call a tycoon with a teenage debutante daughter and I've promised to paint her portrait. But you can come with me. In the old days, we never had the money to take a holiday together. Remember how we used to pore over the travel catalogues and plan trips to Spain or Italy or the Bahamas? Now we'll be able to go everywhere together.'

Miranda drew her knees up, encircling them with her arms. She stared round the firelit studio. She began to think of it as home. It had none of the elegant beauty of John's house – her old home – in Eaton Place. It was magnificently large with a domed ceiling and a skylight, but untidy – a clutter of paints, oils and canvases; a work-room. Yet tonight it seemed to her a real home and full of beauty and warmth.

It was David's hideout and stronghold. She would like it to be hers. She knew she could be happy here, happy in a way that had never been possible with John, despite the luxuries with which he'd always sur-rounded her.

'I'll write to John, my husband, tomorrow – no, perhaps it would be fairer to see him and tell him the truth,' she said. 'I'll make him understand. I'll ask for a divorce, David.'

David walked across the room and pulled on a Paisley silk dressing-gown. He switched on the alabaster lamp by the bookcase, sat down, and smiled at her.

'You do what you think best, Mandy. John is bound to find out sooner or later that you're living with me, so if you want your freedom – you must get it. I only wish to God I could do the same – so that we could be married.'

Miranda felt her heart give one sickening lurch, then to beat furiously as the full impact of those words hit her. How was it possible that she had never thought of this, never once questioned whether or not *David* had remarried? Had he deliberately with-held the facts from her – as Tony had done;

or assumed that she already knew? He had not mentioned a *wife*.

Then she reproached herself swiftly for doubting him.

She alternated between a fierce desire to talk about his wife, and an impulse to get up and run, *run away before it was too late.* But it was too late already. She loved him. Nothing could alter the fact. She couldn't leave him now. She abandoned herself to fate – to him. She said, huskily:

'Tell me about your wife. I want to know.'

'I was married ten years ago. Douna was my model then. We'd been living together for a year, and all that time she was in love with me. She hadn't anybody else in the world but me because her parents had both been killed in the war and she had no other relations. That's why she was so utterly dependent upon me. I wasn't in love with her but grew very attached to her – the way one is to a child who relies on you for security and protection. She was like a little Tanagra figurine – tiny but perfect, with dark hair and almond eyes. I used to tell her she had Burmese blood in her. She had that golden tinge of skin and a thick voluptuous mouth – a painter's joy, in fact.

'That year was a happy one for me. She looked after me and cooked my meals and made life pleasant and comfortable and easy. I took her for granted. I'd no idea she was unhappy until I came home from a dinner and found that she had taken an overdose of sleeping pills. If I'd been an hour later, it would have been too late.'

He moved across the room and sat down on the divan.

'It was a terrible shock. I realized that I'd been damnably selfish, and that it wasn't fair to her. Marrying her seemed the only reasonable solution. She'd let me lead my own life and never curtailed my freedom or interfered with my work. She made few demands on me and marriage seemed so important to her, I went through with it. Douna needed something in place of the love I couldn't give her and we tried hard to have children. She had two miscarriages, then five years ago we had a son. Douna was thrilled and I was pleased for her sake, though I didn't really want the complications of fatherhood. But he was a handsome baby and she worshipped him. She began to live for him, and this somehow made things easier for us both. She no longer counted on me or waited for me in that maddening, pathetic fashion, nor insisted upon going abroad with me. She wouldn't leave Jonathan. She called him that, as a compliment to me – the David of her life! As I saw less of her, I was able to be nicer to her when we *were* together. I put Douna and the baby in this country house in Gerrards Cross. I could afford to make them comfortable, and I did. A daily; a gardener; a car; and so on.'

He broke off and walked across to the window as if he were finding it hard to carry on with the story. When he spoke, his voice was no longer impersonal.

'Jonathan was nearly two when we learned that he was suffering from cerebral palsy. He could never be completely normal but with love and care, and the right medical attention, his condition might improve. What at first had seemed a terrible tragedy began gradually to assume less desperate proportions. There is of course an exceptionally close link between Jonathan and his mother. Oh, he's quite fond of me, too. He looks forward to my visits, and I go and see him and Douna as regularly as I can. She doesn't seem to mind my being away, providing I turn up at reasonable intervals. So you see, Mandy, I couldn't ask for a divorce. I know I could go on visiting Jonathan just the same, but I couldn't bring myself to take away the security which is about all I've been able to give Douna. There has been very little love, but at least she has had me to rely on – to belong to. She knows that however long I may be away, I will go back, and she's told me quite frankly that so long as she is sure I'll never leave her, she is content.'

He turned round now and looked at Miranda almost accusingly.

'You wouldn't want me to destroy that, would you, Mandy?'

She shook her head, mute, unable to trust her voice. She felt devastated. For a moment her imagination was trapped in vivid thoughts of David's wife. It was not David she pitied – not herself – but this other woman; lonely and only half-fulfilled. She, Miranda, ought surely to walk out of David's life; it would be wrong to take something from the other woman who had so small a part of him.

Almost as if in answer to her unspoken thought, David said abruptly:

'Our being together need not affect my marriage. For years now I haven't spent more than the odd weekend at home. If I am too long with Douna and Jonathan, I become irritable and unkind, and it's best for me not to stay more than a day or two. Most of the time you and I could be together, Mandy. Surely that is better than nothing! It's got to be, darling. I just can't go on without you.'

A few hours ago she might have laughed at that cynically. After all, David had managed to get through fifteen years without trying to find her again. But then, so had she, believing, as she had done, that what had once been between them was over. She knew only too well what he meant. Hopelessly in love once more, she could not tolerate the idea of continuing for the rest of her lifetime without him. Must life always be a compromise? she asked herself, bitterly. And then at once chided herself for demanding a full cup of happiness. Some women – Douna for instance – had no more than half a cup. At least *she* would have the one thing in the world that made life worth living – David's love. There must be hundreds of women all around who would never know the real joy of living with the man they loved, and who returned that feeling. A marriage certificate was no guarantee of perpetual happiness, as well she knew. In David's world, convention had never played much of a part; and certainly respectability had never been a guiding star in her own life. Why then be unhappy because David could not marry her? Was it because she knew with absolute certainty that she belonged to him, and to no-one else and so wanted the marriage tie – to complete it?

She realized that David was watching her face, his own taut and anxious. Suddenly, she held out her arms to him and drew him down to her.

'I'll never leave you now,' she said. And if any lingering doubt hovered, as David took her in his arms it was dissolved into nothingness in the searing flame of their renewed desire...

CHAPTER TEN

As Miranda walked into the drawing-room of her home in Eaton Place, John rose at once and came towards her, his hand outstretched. He looked pleased.

'Mandy! So you got my letter. I'm so glad you've come. Glad I was home, too. Another half an hour and I'd have gone back to the office. Why didn't you phone first? I'm not usually here for lunch. We might have missed each other.'

He broke off, seeing the change in that beautiful face. The welcome in his own turned to uncertainty.

'Come and sit down!'

He pulled a comfortable chair towards her and sat down opposite her, waiting for her to speak.

'I didn't get your letter, John. I came on my own initiative because I have to talk to you.'

John relaxed.

'Then we've reached the same conclusion, without influence from each other,' he went on. 'I'm so glad, my dear. At first, my pride forbade me to contact you. Then, as the days and weeks went by and I realized how utterly empty my life was without you, I knew this was one of the occasions in life when pride was of no importance. I want you back. I wrote begging you to return to me.'

Miranda's face was deathly pale now. If she could have found words, she would have interrupted him. But she could hardly make herself realize what he was saying. *He had written suggesting a reconciliation.* He imagined that *this* was why she had come home this afternoon.

She broke out suddenly, her eyes desperate:

'John, don't say any more, please. I never got your letter. I've been abroad quite a bit. I'm afraid you're going to be disappointed. I came – *to ask for a divorce.'*

The last words came out like a pistol shot in the quiet, elegant drawing-room. They seemed to go on reverberating between them until John spoke – thickly now, his expression almost ugly.

'But I wrote to you care of the bank. I was sure they knew where to forward the letter.'

She felt a sudden remorse, combined with a sense of futility. John's letter had been written too late. Perhaps if she had received it before she'd met David again, it might have influenced her. But now it really was too late. She could never go back to the old half-life without real love, or real fulfilment.

Her thoughts swung back to the night she had spent in David's arms. It had been a night of intense passion and assuagement of their mutual desire. How happy they both had been, waking later, their bodies still entwined. How tenderly David had kissed her into wakefulness and boyishly happy, he had cooked breakfast for her, bringing it to her, eating it with her in the big divan bed.

'Why do you want a divorce? Have you met someone else? Someone you want to marry!'

John's voice, harsh and stilted, brought her back to the present. Her hands twisted together in her lap.

'It's not that, John. I've met David again. I'm going to live with him. I love him and he loves me and I intend to stay with him now for always.'

John's face was grey, convulsed. He breathed unevenly, stood up and began to pace the room.

'I've often wondered if you'd really got over that first marriage. I'm not a fool, Mandy. During the years you lived with me, you never quite belonged to me; never gave me all of yourself. I realized damn well that something was missing. Admit it, all the time you were in my life, you went on loving *him*.'

She was stung to defend herself.

'That isn't true! I almost hated him at

first. I felt he'd let me down and that it was all over – for always. I didn't cheat you, John. I wanted to love you – to be everything to you and let you be the same to me. Somehow, it just didn't work out – that's all.'

He stopped pacing and stared down at her, his lips a thin, straight line.

'So you want to remarry him!'

Miranda bit her lip.

'Well, no. As a matter of fact, he has a wife. For various reasons I won't go into now, he can't get a divorce. I'm asking you for my freedom because I want to be able to start my own life again without feeling responsible to anyone else. I imagined you might even welcome your freedom and perhaps marry again...' She added those words a trifle lamely.

'I'm not divorcing you, Miranda!'

She looked up at him, shocked and appalled.

'But, John, you were quite willing for us to separate. Divorce is only one step further. You're not against divorce on a matter of principle, I know. You've often said you believed it was best for people who couldn't live together happily. Why won't you set me free?'

He gave a wry smile.

'At least you pay me a compliment by not suggesting I am refusing your request out of spite. No, it's quite simple. I know you

Mandy – perhaps better than you know your-self. Living with a man – half a life you call it – won't make you happy. What you choose to call "love" can't last in such surroundings. Sooner or later, you'll leave David again. Why set you free just to make another mistake?'

She stood up, her face flushed with anger.

'How can you judge what David and I feel for each other? I'm happy with him, John, in a way I never was with you. He understands me and I understand him. We're like one person when we are together. Because it broke up once is no proof that it won't last this time. We were both desperately young and egotistical – too young to be tolerant, or to appreciate what we had. This time it will be different.'

'Will it? Are *you* really different? Has *he* really changed? Apparently he isn't willing to give up everything for you despite this great love, or he'd agree to divorce his wife. Are you really willing to share him with someone else? To be content, knowing that every time you sleep with him, or cook a meal for him, or take his suit to the cleaners, you are stealing those rights from another? Not you, Mandy. Just now you are blind to the truth – in love, like a foolish schoolgirl. You see only what you want to see. But you're really too honest, too conventional a person at heart, to want that sort of exist-ence. It couldn't last. You'd grow to loathe it and David – and then...'

He broke off, suddenly unsure of himself. Why was he fighting for Miranda? Was he willing to wait and pick up the pieces a second time? He'd never been a violently jealous man and yet now he was appalled by the thought of his wife – *his wife* – in her former husband's arms, giving herself and her glorious body, her mind, her heart, to someone else. Yet she had at one time been David's wife, too. And there had been other men – he'd never asked about them. After they had become engaged and she had admitted she had had other lovers, he'd told her he didn't want to know about them. Somehow, despite the life she had led, she seemed so uncorrupted, innocent in a way he couldn't explain but could appreciate. She was not wanton – she was physically passionate, yet it was a desire for love, not sex, which motivated her.

Trying to sort it all out now, he thought that it might not have been easy for her to distinguish one from the other since her immediate appeal to men was invariably sexual. Other men had wanted her, swept her off her feet and claimed her for a while, just as he had done. But they, too, had been unable to hold her.

'I won't divorce you!' he said again, and his face was harder than she had thought possible. This was a John she did not recognize. 'Go and live with David if you must, I won't try to stop you. But at least, think about it first. Lead this new existence with him but not in a haze of romantic illusion. You aren't a young girl any more, Mandy, you're a woman. You ought to have more sense. Oh, I understand that our life together – yours and mine – failed to answer some need in you. But don't rush off into this liaison with David just because you don't know what else to do with your life. Come back to me for a while – why don't you? – and think it all over quietly and calmly, right away from his influence. I won't make any demands on you. You can live in this house as though we were friends and no more. If you like, I'll even move into my club for a few weeks. But I do want you to be quite sure this time.'

She was surprised – even touched. But she knew what he suggested was impossible. Even now, while he was talking, she yearned to get back to David, to that studio, to *love*. She knew she couldn't consider John's suggestion.

'It's no use, John!' she said gently. 'I really do love David. I must go to him. Now – at once. But thank you.'

John walked away from her and stood staring out of the window, his face suddenly aged. There were lines of pain about his mouth and pain in his eyes – an expression that he hid from her. He loathed being helpless, defeated, and pitiable.

Fool, fool! he chided himself mercilessly. You had her and you lost her. You wanted so much.

Even the incompleteness of their marriage had seemed preferable to losing her altogether. He should never have agreed to their original separation, or given her freedom in which to find someone else. Women didn't appreciate consideration. They wanted to be swept off their feet, made to do things they didn't know they wanted. If only he, John, had been stronger, more forceful with her. If – if – *if*–

His face twisted into a bitter grimace. A tower of strength was something *he'd* never be. Too proud, perhaps! Yet at the time Miranda had left he had meant merely to be considerate. Was it just that he was weak? Where Miranda was concerned, yes – he had wanted to give her everything she wanted. Was that why their marriage had failed? Ought he to have taken, as well as given so much? Women said they had to feel *needed*. Perhaps Miranda hadn't realized his need of her, so often left unexpressed, or repressed because he hadn't been sure *she* wanted *him*.

Miranda stared round the room. She knew she must get up and go and yet felt unable to make the final move. She didn't want to hurt John – the one who had been so very good to her. It would have been easier if she could have hated him, but she didn't – no one could hate John. She was still fond of him just as she had always been. Loving David did not detract from that particular affection, any more than being kind to Douna detracted from what David gave *her*, Miranda. With David she shared an urgent, demanding, all-absorbing passion and love. With John she had shared only companionship, a surface association really – a quiet affection. But it had been devoid of the brilliant, breathless colour and excitement she experienced with David.

'Let me go, John!' she said, her voice only just audible.

He turned round and looked at her, his face now expressionless.

'You will leave of your own accord, if you go; not with my blessing. I will never divorce you.'

There was nothing more to be said.

She turned and left him standing there like a figure turned to stone, as she went out of the room.

For a few minutes, her heart was torn with pity. Almost she turned back and told him that it was not the end of the world; that she was sure he would make a life without her and be all the happier for it. But as she opened the front door and stepped into the bright spring sunshine, her thoughts winged away from the house that had been her home, and rushed in ecstasy towards the future – the future with David, the new life and the old love that fantastically and irrevocably had come to reclaim her.

CHAPTER ELEVEN

'It's sweet of you to stay, Sue. I don't know how I'd have got through this weekend without you.'

Miranda's friend flung her arms over her head in an effort to find a cool breath of air in the studio room. It was very hot up here with the July sun burning down through the huge window. It was a week of heat-wave. Even with the skylights open, the sun seemed to consume the last vestige of air.

They had spent the day in the park, under the trees, along with most of North London's population. Had it been any cooler in Sue's flat, Sue would have suggested they went back there. Here at least there was a faint breeze off the park. Besides, Miranda clung to this room like a child sheltering in its familiar nursery – afraid to face the world outside.

Sue regarded Miranda with anxiety. She looked terribly thin and pale. There were shadows beneath her eyes and an expression in them which frightened her. Those beautiful, clear blue eyes held an almost animal look of fear.

'What *is* wrong, Mandy?' she broke the

silence between them. 'I don't want to press for confidences if you don't want to give them, but there's something almost desperate about you. It's not a bit like you. You've lost all your humour and gaiety. I long to help. I can't if I don't know what's hit you.'

Miranda lay across the top of the divan bed she shared with David. Her eyes were closed now. Her arms hung limply at her sides. At Sue's words, the ready tears glistened for a moment on the thick, gold-tipped lashes, before spilling down her cheeks. Roughly, she wiped them away with the back of her arm. May be it *would* help to tell Sue. No woman had ever had a better friend and anything she said to Sue would remain secret.

'It isn't any one thing – it's lots of them,' she said desperately.

She sat up and looked at Sue now with a kind of despair written on her face.

'I thought it would be so easy. I thought I could share David with his work, his wife and his child. I thought so long as we really loved each other, nothing else would matter. But it does, it does! I'm afraid, Sue, I'm afraid.'

'But of what? David loves you, doesn't he?'

'Yes, he loves me. But he has two lives which are of equal importance. His work – I've always known that was important, of course. Sometimes he gets up at six in the morning and starts to paint, and for the rest of the day, perhaps for three or four days on end, I don't exist for him. I can bear that. I understand it these days. But there's that *other* life. She, Douna, has only to ring up and say that the child has a cold or he's not well – no matter how trivial a thing – and he's off like a flash. I shouldn't be jealous – I'm not really. I know she can never leave the child. But it hurts. No matter what we'd planned to do, David just sweeps it to one side and rushes off. He seems to think it doesn't matter to me – takes it for granted I'll understand. In a way I do, but each time he goes I feel humiliated, even cheapened. It's as if he's forcing me to realize that I'm only his mistress like Douna used to be; without security; legal rights; any kind of hold, really.'

'God, darling, and you're the one who used to deplore "legal rights" and all that,' exclaimed Sue in a shocked voice.

'I know. One changes before one has time to realize it. That's what humiliates me – my own craven longing for security all of a sudden. I think it's because I love and need David so much. That's what Douna wanted and she got it – but I didn't.'

'Then why don't you leave him?'

'Because I can't. I'm still crazy about him – more so than when we first started living together again. I want to be his wife, to have his children. When I'm alone I think about Melanie. Then I remember Jonathan. I'm all mixed up – tortured – can't you see it?'

Sue did see it. She was thoroughly worried now – startled by the unaccustomed hysteria in Miranda. She poured out a whisky and water and gave it to her friend.

Miranda gulped down a few mouthfuls and continued:

'I've got to admit that David doesn't seem to need me now as he did a few months ago. Then he couldn't bear me out of his sight. I had to sit beside him while he worked so that he could talk to me. If I went out, he insisted on coming with me. I was his shadow, and he was mine. Now he has become physically satiated. It's the nature of the male, isn't it, for sexual desire to diminish? But his need for me as a person seems less, too. I can't bear that. Perhaps it would be better if I got a job. I haven't really enough to do in the studio. My personal life is nil, except during the times when David is with me. He doesn't want me to work. He wants me to be here ready and waiting when he needs me. But I'm as restless as a cat. Every moment is precious, and I don't want to waste it. I've already lost so many years of him, I can't afford to lose even a second more. Is it mad to love a man so much? Even David, my perfect lover, isn't as obsessed as I am.'

Sue shrugged her shoulders.

'It's unwise! I don't think anyone can live perpetually at fever heat. Men certainly don't like such constant emotional tension. Somehow you've *got* to learn to relax Mandy, and get things into proportion. I don't think I've ever realized quite how emotional you are. You always appear so cool, so calm, so controlled. Yet underneath you are such a wild, impassioned, reckless creature. I'm worried stiff about you, darling.'

Miranda tried to smile.

'Aren't all women wild and impassioned and reckless when they are really in love? I'd do anything in the world for David – anything. The only thing I can't do is give him up.'

'Has he ever hinted he'd like you to?'

'Oh, no! At least, I don't think so. But sometimes when I'm left alone here and he's with Douna, I wonder if I just make life more complicated for him than it was. He's torn between two conflicting loyalties. He knows how I feel when he's away and yet he has to go to Douna and the boy. I can't hide my disappointment and I suppose there are times when he resents being made to feel remorseful about me. But I'll tell you something David doesn't and never *will* know. I went to see his wife and child.'

'You *what?*' Sue cried, and held her glass suspended on the way to her lips.

'Yes! I didn't, of course, tell them who I

was. I pretended to be someone from TV doing a census. I had to know what Douna was really like – if she is as helpless – as hopeless as David makes her seem – dependent on him. I thought perhaps she might really be just a clever woman who was playing her cards right so that she would get him completely in the end.'

'And was she?'

Miranda shook her head.

'No! She's gentle and rather sweet. She has enormous, pathetic brown eyes; not much personality and her figure isn't good. She's quite plump now. She has no elegance – no taste. Provincial describes her best, I think. The house is the same – the kind one sees a hundred times – full of arty-crafty chintzes and candlewick bedspreads and multi-coloured stair-carpets. Do I sound patronising? I don't mean to. I'm just trying to put you in the picture. But David is marvellous. He loathes her décor and just allows her to do as she wishes. It is *her* home. She showed me David's photograph on the mantelpiece, and for the first time since I'd entered the house, she came really alive. Yes, she loves him, Sue. And yes, he *is* her life. The great man. The great painter. Her god. I hated her for it, yet pitied her at the same time.'

'And the child?'

Miranda's face twisted a little at the memory.

238

'Jonathan is like a miniature David with his high cheekbones and narrow eyes. I almost gave myself away and remarked on it when the boy came into the room. It nearly broke my heart to see those thin little legs encased in callipers. Sue, he's the baby I hoped to have when I found David again; not in callipers but a perfect replica of my David. Ever since I've seen Jonathan I've been filled with the desperate longing to have another child. I know it's madness – impossible, as David and I are not married, but reason doesn't enter into it. Sometimes when we're making love, I feel a positively bitter resentment of David because he won't let me conceive. Not that he knows I want a child. I think he'd be horrified if I told him.'

'Why don't you?'

'Because I don't think he'd understand. He told me once when he was talking about Jonathan that he would never have another child and risk the same pain of having to watch it grow up handicapped, like Jonathan. Besides, he hasn't time for another child. He's torn in too many directions already. And then, too, there is the risk that Douna might found out and be hurt. He wouldn't do anything to hurt her deliberately. He feels a kind of protectiveness towards her that comes very close to love.'

'My poor Mandy!'

'I'm trapped!' Miranda said in a tragic

239

voice. 'I walked into this with both eyes open and yet I never quite imagined what it would mean. You know, I think John sensed something of this. Strange, really, as I never considered him a perceptive man. But he warned me I wouldn't fine true happiness this way. I suppose I want too much. *That's* always been my downfall, Sue.'

'You know I saw John the other day?' Sue remarked. 'He came over to our place and asked me quite openly if I had news of you. When I said you'd been on the telephone the previous week, he fairly plied me with questions. What were you doing? Where were you living? Did you seem happy? Did I know if you were going out of London for the summer? He's still in love with you, poor old John.'

'Is he? I hope not, for his sake. I doubt it, Sue. John isn't the kind of man to pursue the unobtainable. He's ruled by logic – not by his heart.'

'How can you be sure? He looked desperately unhappy. Pete and I felt rather sorry for him.'

Miranda turned from her friend's soft, reproachful gaze.

'Don't – please don't!' she said sharply. 'I don't want to be made to feel guilty about John.'

'I wasn't trying to make you feel that. I was only trying to show you that there *is* a way out of this–' she waved her arm around the studio. 'John would take you back, I'm sure of that. You were happy with him once – perhaps you could be again.'

'No, no! You just don't understand, Sue. Life with John was only an existence. Each day passed, pleasantly enough but without any real meaning, or purpose. It was a *day*, no more. A day with David is a lifetime in itself. I forget the rest of the world. I live for David. When he is with me I am utterly fulfilled. These depressions come down on me like a kind of migraine when I'm alone. *With* him, I'm tremendously happy – content in a way I never could be with John. The tiniest things bring me joy – one look, one word of praise from David; our shared appreciation of music, of art, a glimpse from that window, all those tiny things. We share every emotion. We are like one person. I'm part of him and he is part of me. To be without him again would be death to me. I'd never survive it.'

The room was growing cooler as the last glimmer of sun disappeared in the tender twilight. Miranda got up, found a white wool cardigan, and threw it over her bare shoulders.

'Another month, and summer will be over!' she said irrelevantly, filled with a terrible sadness. Then she shook her head, smiled and her face became young and alive again as she added:

'Next week we're going down to the Cornish coast – just David and me – to a remote village where there is a fantastic castle on the cliffs near Tintagel – a relic of King Arthur's days – restored and made into a home by a wealthy manufacturer. He has offered David a fabulous sum to paint his young daughter, and to stay in this romantic castle. David said he was bringing "his wife" so for a few weeks at least I shall feel we are a married couple again. David has been there and says it is glorious, overlooking a marvellous stretch of sands and rocks and with the sea thundering up the cliff-side at high tide, right below the castle windows. Except that David has to work, it'll seem like a honeymoon for us. I'll write and tell you all about it, Sue. I'll write you long newsy descriptive letters while David works.'

But those letters were never written.

They went down to Cornwall. Miranda, as well as David, was given a warm welcome by the owner of the castle – Mark Correlly. He was a grey-haired, vital man who had made a fortune out of steel. He was self-educated, still vigorous at the age of fifty, and a doting father because he had married late and his wife had died in child-birth. Deborah was all he had. He had bought and restored the Cornish castle for her, because she loved the sea. His sister, Miss Agnes

Correlly, ran the place with a large staff – a few natives of the Cornish village – and a dozen foreigners. Money was no object. The place had been furnished in lavish style by a specialist in décor who had made it lovely in an imaginative way, which appealed to the artist in David as well as to Miranda.

As a rule, David refused to go to clients' houses to paint. He preferred the sitting to be in his own studio, but the offer from Mr Correlly had been too tempting. Besides, in this heat-wave it was wonderfully cool facing the shining green-blue waters of the Atlantic.

There was not much of a garden. The winds blew too hard and too often, but there was a private swimming pool; meals on the terrace, music, a handsome library, and some pictures which David would have liked to have owned. He and Miranda were given a suite with an enormous bedroom which led into a kind of tower with circular windows looking right down into the sea.

All day, David painted in a summer-house in the garden. There was plenty of light there and he could be quiet and undisturbed. Miranda experienced at first all the rapture that she had anticipated of a second honey-moon, and the thrill of being called 'Mrs Leyland' again. At night they lay in each other's arms in a big four-poster bed, listening to the hiss of the waves lashing against the rocks below their open window, breathing in the cool, salty air. It was romantic and inspiring. In the daytime, while David worked, she had plenty of time to take walks and grow sunburned and feel strong and well again. But gradually it was all spoiled. The sight of that summer-house and the knowledge that *he* was down there with Deborah, devastated her. The young girl was surprisingly attractive with the Titian red hair beloved by the Venetian painters and the milk-white skin that went with it. She had a small impudent face with a tilted nose dusted with golden freckles, and twinkling greenish eyes. There was a velvet-brown mole on her left cheek. She was always deploring it, but David had told her in front of Miranda that it was one of nature's 'most perfect imperfections', a beauty spot, and he would paint it; he was painting her with her long red hair unbound and in a plain green tunic dress, very short, showing her beautiful sun-browned legs and bare feet. She was a nymph, a dryad, a Sea King's daughter, he said. The poetic images that he thought up for her were endless.

Miranda was afraid to write to Sue, and at the end of the second week she gave up all efforts to do so. She was once more a harassed, dejected, frightened woman. But Deborah was young and innocent and as full of fun as a kitten and she was always laughing. She made David laugh. It drove

Miranda mad to hear their laughter.

At last she wrote as if she were keeping an intimate diary for herself – from her desperate, aching heart.

'Jealousy is an ugly thing. It makes everything ugly, too. It makes me as ugly and old as she is young and beautiful. I cannot blame David for being fascinated by the girl. Deborah Correlly has everything – her looks, her vital charm and all the virginal sweetness of an eighteen-year-old; a sweetness that David has already cruelly told me, made him think of me as I used to be. I believe he is half in love with her already. If it weren't for me – his supposed wife – I think she would have encouraged him, and he would be head over heels in love by now, as only a painter of David's calibre can be. Beauty-loving, sensitive to women of all ages, he never takes his eyes off her – even during meals I watch him staring at her. He knows I've noticed, and of course tried to tell me that it's only the artist in him which admires her. Maybe he believes it. I know him better ... I know because of the way he makes love to me at night when we are at last alone; she lies there, too, in the back of his mind. And in mine. Oh, God, in mine!'

Miranda stopped writing, unable to express in words how she felt when David made love to her these days. It was almost as if he were *willing* her to be Deborah, the young, seductive Deborah. He used to love her, Miranda, with his eyes as well as his hands and body, she thought; now his eyes are always shut and he lies tense and rigid. Was he pretending all the time that it was Deborah who lay in his arms? Was her own tenseness responsible for the failure to find the usual pleasure in their love-making? She thought so but could not prevent it. She had wondered, lying sleepless and terribly alone by David's side, if he guessed what was wrong. Several times she had tried to talk to him. Anything – even a quarrel would be better than this growing estrangement. But the words wouldn't come and David either refused to speak, or dared not do so. So the game of pretence went on.

She turned once more to her writing pad. The ability which had made her such a good journalist made it possible for her to find some release in putting her thoughts on paper.

'Am I imagining all this?' she wrote. *'Does David still love me as much as ever? Maybe his admiration for Deborah is no more than that of an artist in love with sheer virginal beauty for its own sake. Or perhaps he feels paternal about her. But that's wishful thinking! He told me that he could only love when his mind was also fascinated – that's why he painted me so often … because he loved me.'*

Last month, she had longed for this holiday in Cornwall. Now, perversely, she longed to go back to London – to the hot, breathless, untidy studio, sitting for David, knowing that all his thoughts were concentrated upon *her* as a model. She had grumbled then to Sue because she had to share him with his work and his wife and child. Now it was worse, sharing him with a young, exquisite girl.

It won't last – it can't! she told herself wretchedly. As soon as we leave, he'll forget all about Deborah. Ought I to go home and leave him alone for this last week? Perhaps he would love me more if I could let him go. Where is my courage now? My pride? *I dare not go because I don't trust him!*

While she was writing, the sound of Deborah's laughter came floating across the sun-drenched garden from the summer-house. The childlike happiness of the laugh tore at Miranda's heart. In it was all the excitement and discovery of life and new first love – of adventure, awakening. What had she to offer David that could compete with Deborah's fresh youth and dazzling beauty?

'It's so easy for her,' she thought bitterly. 'She has never known poverty, hardship, pain or disillusion. I can't laugh like that now even when I am happy. Once I did, in those early days of my marriage to David.

Was I mad to think I could recapture the simple sweetness of that first love? It never lasts. The bright crystal will always cloud over in time, after a man and woman live in close intimacy. Hasn't David learned this, too, or is he trying now to recapture his own joyous youth and illusions? Maybe without them he couldn't paint? He needs laughter.'

She sighed uneasily. Since she had been living with him, she had been too serious – too intense. He had known of her sadness, her inner loneliness; sensed it even though she had not spoken of it; resented it, perhaps. Somehow she should have hidden it all – and yet, what woman can live with a man she loves and not be herself sometimes? There was a kind of pagan pride about a woman's love – *Here I am, as I am; take me if you will, all that I am and am not. Love me as I am, with my faults and my failures and my weakness, as well as my virtues. Make of me what you will.*

'I cannot leave him!' she thought, her mind suddenly calm, accepting its fate. 'Only if he tells me he doesn't want me any more will I go. I left him once but I haven't the courage or the will to do so again. Whatever I suffer, I must stay with him while he has any need of me at all. And once we leave Cornwall, he will need me again. When we are back in the studio, he will forget Deborah – he will be all mine again.'

248

But she knew she would not forget. It must be part of the price of living. She had told John with such conviction that she had to live at all costs. Now, indeed, she was living and paying the price of love, and it was almost unbearably high!

CHAPTER TWELVE

'Good God, Mandy, it was only a kiss!'

David's face was sulky, his voice irritable. Miranda fought to keep her self-control. She kept trying to see things from David's point of view, but always clouding the issue was the picture of Deborah, young, appealing, lovely, clasped in David's arms; on her face a look of utter rapture. And David's face absorbed, flushed and equally abandoned.

A kiss sounded harmless, perhaps, but some instinct warned her that after she had left the summer-house the kiss might have led to something more. Miranda wanted to believe David more than anything in the world. She wanted to be quite sure that this was utterly unimportant and did not in any way touch upon his love for her. They had neither of them seen her. She went quickly away, swearing to herself that she would never let David know that she had found them together. He despised anything ugly. There was nothing more ugly than a jealous woman. She knew that.

But for the remaining few days of their stay they had been like strangers, and they had drawn no nearer to each other once they got back to the studio. That was three days ago.

Tomorrow, David was off for the weekend to Gerrards Cross, and Miranda's iron resolve to say nothing of what she had seen had slowly weakened until she knew she could not endure those two days alone unless the constraint between them was cleared up once and for all.

David was putting some finishing touches to the magnificent portrait he had done of Deborah. Looking over his shoulder, the artist in Miranda admired the sparkling freshness of the young face so cleverly reproduced in oils, but the words sprang to her lips and cut across the silence between them.

'Are you in love with her?'

He turned and stared at her; his face red and sullen.

'You're behaving like a schoolgirl, Mandy. Surely you've passed the age when one believes that a man must be in love with every girl he kisses.'

She was stung to reply:

'You once told me that you had to be a little in love with your model if the painting was to be a success. This...' She pointed to the nymph-like figure outlined against the Cornish rocks. '...this is one of the most compelling portraits you've ever painted.'

For a moment, David was silent. His gaze fastened on the outline of Deborah's cheek

– the soft yet firm curve of her small breasts.

'She was very beautiful.'

The words were not so much addressed to Miranda as to himself.

Miranda turned away, her eyes suddenly stung by hot tears. She felt utterly helpless and alone. She felt that she couldn't fight against this. She'd always known that David's work came first and that his work and his private life were inextricably bound together. If she was to find peace of mind, she must learn to accept such episodes as this – to leave David free in the way that his wife had done. But it wasn't easy – particularly for anyone like herself for whom love is total and all-absorbing. If she herself only had outside interests – hobbies, a job, children – then every facet of her relationship with David might not be of such vital importance.

Commonsense told her that it was wrong to concentrate so exclusively upon any human being, but her essential nature undermined her logic.

'Very well, forget it!'

Her voice was deliberately casual. She went across and stood behind David. He sat perched on a three-legged stool in front of the easel. She rested her arms lightly on his shoulders and laid her cheek against his hair.

'You ought to be flattered, darling, to know that I am jealous even of a kiss.'

'Of course I'm flattered but really, Mandy,

you've absolutely no cause to be jealous. You know it's you I love. Nothing in the world is as important to me as your happiness. I'd do anything in the world for you.'

It isn't true. Her mind rejected the glib promises, even as her heart reached out eagerly to his comfort.

'I wish you hadn't to go home tomorrow!'

She bit back the words, realizing that once again she was trying to put chains around him. The smile had already left his face. His forehead creased in a frown.

'But of course I understand,' she added, hastily. 'Try to get back Sunday night if you can, darling. I'll have something special for supper.'

He relaxed again and stood up, stretching his arms lazily above his head.

'I think we should go somewhere special tonight. I'll take you to the *Empress*. Did I tell you that Deborah's father insisted upon giving me a cheque when I said good-bye? I told him there was no need until I sent the portrait but he insisted. He seemed absolutely delighted with it. He wants me to do another in the New Year, when Deborah comes out. He says he'd like to have a more formal painting – you know the kind of thing, debutante's ball-dress, long white gloves and so on. I think she'd look enchanting...' He broke off, realizing that perhaps the subject was not in the best of taste.

'We'll really go to town tonight,' he went on with a fresh burst of enthusiasm. 'You know I agreed to do this portrait for three hundred? Well, the old boy insisted upon adding another hundred. Not that he'll notice the difference. Deborah told me he's not far off being a millionaire. I'm going to buy you a present, Mandy. What would you like? A piece of jewellery, I think. Shall I give you a ring, darling – an eternity ring, perhaps?'

She was in his arms now, tender, yielding to his sudden, spontaneous show of affection.

'I still have your engagement ring, David,' she said.

But she couldn't bring herself to add that she had kept his wedding ring, too. At the time, she had felt rather stupid for being sentimental, but now she was glad.

'Fancy keeping the old engagement ring,' David said, but he sounded pleased. 'If I remember, it only cost about thirty pounds and the diamond was so small you needed a magnifying glass to see it.'

By the time he'd married Douna, of course, he'd been able to afford something very much more extravagant. Yes, he must give Miranda something really good this time. It couldn't have been much fun for her in Cornwall. Maybe when he went down to Tintagel next time it would be better to leave her behind.

He could not admit to himself that this would not be so much for her sake as his own. Her moodiness had been a constant brake and had made him fidgety and ill at ease. Poor darling Miranda was so emotional, so intense! But he didn't really wish her to be different; particularly not when they were here together, at home. Her concentration, her devotion, flattered and stimulated him. He knew that she'd given up quite a lot in the way of luxurious living when she moved in with him. However, he didn't want to be made to feel guilty about it. After all, she had come to live with him of her own free will and he wasn't responsible for her – not the way he would have been responsible if he'd had an affair with Deborah. Just as well Miranda had been there to stop that little episode developing. The old boy mightn't have been at all pleased if he, David, had seduced the apple of Papa's eye.

David grinned and went into the bathroom to run the bath for Miranda. Presently, he would pour in the essence for her – 'Misouka' – pungent, rather Eastern. They both liked it and he would sit on the stool while she lay in the water. They would sip their drinks and chat for a while until the water got too cool, then he would dry her in one of the big fleecy bath towels and take her through to the bedroom, and make love to her. Afterwards, they would go out and enjoy their evening. Life was good, he thought. He was quite content...

On Sunday night, David telephoned her to say he would not be home after all. Miranda's carefully-prepared meal was completely wasted. Sheer disappointment made it impossible for her to eat a thing herself.

Jonathan wasn't too well, was his explanation, and Douna wanted him to stay and be with her on Monday when the doctor called.

'I'll ring you Monday lunchtime and give you an update!' David said. He sounded quite cheerful.

But Miranda spent a miserable night alone, trying to concentrate on a light romantic novel that she had taken to bed. Unfortunately, the inevitable happy ending became apparent before she had read more than half the book and she put it down in disgust.

Life wasn't like this book – it didn't always hold a simple solution and turn out all for the best. The only really happily-married couple she knew was Sue and Peter, and then Sue had admitted that much as she adored Peter, it wasn't in the desperate and frantic way that Miranda loved David. Often Sue and Peter quarrelled, then made it up again like children. Neither would have dreamt of being unfaithful. But to Miranda such love sounded more like a satisfactory, affectionate relationship with an occasional hour or two of sex to highlight the relationship.

Sue doesn't feel as deeply, as completely as I do, Miranda thought. She is never either right up or right down – her nature is calm and placid, and so is Peter's. How easy life must be if one can live that kind of life and like it.

John was the same. For a while, even she, Miranda, had succeeded in accepting what each day brought without questions or criticism. Loving in the way she loved David, left no room for quiet acceptance.

Miranda picked up a book of poems and turned to one by Sidney Lysaght called *The Penalty of Love.* How well he expressed the pain and loneliness as well as the joys of love! Strangely enough, loneliness was one of the main troubles. Because she desired so terribly to be one with David, merged with him mentally and physically, she was constantly aware of this spiritual isolation in which, she supposed, most human beings lived. Only in brief moments, rare and maddeningly elusive, could she cease to be herself and became part of the man she loved. During all the thousands of seconds in the day, Miranda was sharply aware of being completely alone – a prisoner of her own emotions.

On Monday, David telephoned again to say he could not return to the studio for at least three days. Little Jonathan had a high temperature. David was a bit worried. Douna was so helpless. He must stay with them.

The three days became a week. Miranda began to dread the sound of the telephone bell even while she stayed in the studio, afraid to go out in case she should miss a call from David. Another weekend passed. Now the boy had pneumonia and David said Douna was distraught and he could not leave.

'Frightfully sorry, darling! But I know you'll understand.'

Yes, she understood – how could she not when her own baby – their baby – had died from the same illness? She would have been the first to criticize David if he'd neglected his wife and son in such a crisis; but at the same time, she understood more clearly than ever what living with David meant. Complete self-abnegation. A rigid control of her feelings which she was not sure she could maintain.

She went out now – to shop, for long walks in Hyde Park, to museums, to the cinema – to anything that might fill in the hours and help her forget her loneliness. She felt cut off from the rest of the world. It was as though the people milling round her were not real and that she alone was alive and suffering among the crowds.

She drank innumerable cups of coffee, but ate practically nothing and realized that if she went on like this, she would get ill. Once, she went round to Sue's flat but at the last moment turned away, afraid of the sympathetic understanding her friend might offer – afraid of *pity*.

She was near to breaking point when David finally came home. He arrived unexpectedly after ten days absence. She flung herself into his arms, laughing and crying together, with surprise, with joy and relief.

'I've missed you so terribly. You don't know what it's been like, David. I think the nights were the worst – they never seemed to end. You're looking so tired, my darling. Sit down and I'll get you something to eat and drink. Oh, David, it's so marvellous to have you back.'

He kissed her, then drew away. He looked haggard and preoccupied.

'I've missed you, too, sweet. Unfortunately, I won't have time for a meal. I've only rushed back to collect some shirts and another suit. I must go in about half an hour. Has the laundry come back? I brought the dirty stuff with me. It can go off on Thursday, can't it?'

It was a moment or two before Miranda could trust herself to speak. Her heart seemed to plunge. She felt quite sick.

'Is Jonathan worse?'

David shook his head.

'Oh, no! Miles better – well on the way to recovery, I'm glad to say. But he's still in hospital and I promised Douna I'd go back to her. I can't let her stay there alone in that house.'

Alone! Miranda's mind fastened on the word. Why – it was almost funny that he should have used *that* word, she thought, with bitterness that was close to hysteria. Could any woman's loneliness compare with what *she* had been through these last ten days? Why should David be considerate to one woman and not to another? Just because Douna was his wife, did that mean that she, Miranda, had less right to his compassion? Was he so blind that he couldn't sense her complete and absolute despair?

'How long do you think you'll have to stay with Douna?' She asked the question quietly but her feelings were indescribably bitter and hopeless.

David rummaged through his chest of drawers, pulling out an assortment of things. He flung a bundle of clean shirts and socks on the bed, then turned to Miranda, shrugging his shoulders.

'A week – perhaps two. I'll be back as soon as I can. I say, darling, why don't you get out of town? This heat is stifling and you look terribly off-colour. Why not go down to

Brighton or Eastbourne or somewhere – get a breath of sea air? It would do you good.'

Her mind concentrated for a moment on the picture he summoned – of herself, one among the hot, perspiring crowds that seethe along the Brighton front and crowd the hotels, the beaches and the streets. Miranda – one of them, lost and even more lonely than before; sick, *sick* with loneliness. But Douna mustn't be alone.

'I don't like crowds.'

David glanced at her irritably. Miranda was obviously in one of her moods. He was too centred in his own worries to be tolerant.

'Then why not go somewhere quiet? Cornwall or...' he broke off, remembering that young Deborah lived in Cornwall. His face suddenly brightened.

'Tell you what, darling, why not come with me? It's glorious in our garden. I'll introduce you as a casual friend and Douna won't suspect anything. She's completely without guile or jealousy. The perfect temperament–' he added on a slightly reproachful note.

Miranda was appalled by this suggestion. Her life might not have been particularly conventional but there were limits to the lengths to which she would go in order to be with a man she loved. His idea seemed to her quite disgraceful. He must have seen and understood the disapproval registered on her face, for he said, defensively:

'I don't see why you're shocked by that suggestion. You've often told me that you despise conventionality.'

He turned away from her, flung his suitcase on the bed and began to pack.

'I can't think why you choose to "live in sin" with me, if that is your attitude to life.'

'But I love you!' The words were out before she could stop them. 'I can't feel it's sinful. We were once married, anyhow.'

He pushed a couple of pairs of socks into a corner of his suitcase and snapped:

'Love – it's all you think about and you don't even think logically or consistently. If you love me all that much, you'd be willing to come with me no matter where I went. What's more, you'd want to make life easier for me instead of more difficult...'

'David, I do. Oh, please don't let's start a quarrel. You'll be leaving me in a minute.'

'I wasn't starting a quarrel. You were the one who complained about disliking being left here on your own. I suggested you should come down to Gerrards Cross with me and you didn't like that, either. So what *do* you want?'

Time swung backwards and the fifteen years were wiped out. Melanie had been dead for little over a year. As now, Miranda was distraught, lonely and desperately in need of David's love; then, too, he had looked at her with just the same expression of incomprehension and irritation; spoken as he did now using the same voice, those self-same words:

'*So what do you want?*'

Another chance, another child, understanding. But how could one put into words what a woman needed from a man, and how could one demand something from him which he was not capable of giving? David's conception of love was different in the final analysis from her own. For him, it meant a stimulating and satisfying sexual union – little else.

But sex alone isn't enough for me, Miranda thought in despair.

David was already beginning to regret what he had said. He came across the room and put his arms around her.

'You're quite right, darling. It really is silly to quarrel. Mad, too. We've wasted a whole hour when we could have been in bed, and now there isn't time.'

He grinned at her charmingly, boyishly, ruefully. 'Never mind, sweet. We'll make up for it the moment I get back again. Now I really must go or I'll miss that train, and I did promise Douna I'd be on it. If you change your mind about coming down – give me a ring.'

He kissed her on the mouth. For a moment she was unable to respond, then she clung to him fiercely, returning his kiss, her arms holding him so tightly that he had to use force to break away from her.

She watched him walk away across the room, lift his hand in a quick farewell wave, then disappear, smiling, through the studio door. No matter what happened to David, it was never long before he was able to smile again. His resilience was astonishing. No doubt when he finally returned from Gerrards Cross and found she had left him, he would be horrified and hurt. But he would soon recover his good spirits. There'd be some other girl – someone who was light-hearted and casual and easy – not someone who was looking for the heights and depths of love.

Miranda moved around the room, collecting her belongings and packing them slowly and meticulously in the expensive suitcases which John had bought for her. Her eyes were dry – the hurt went too deep for tears; but her face was a taut mask of pain. This time, parting with David was not only difficult and painful because of lost love, but because of the disillusionment *in love itself.*

She had known passion with other men in her life, but her heart had remained intact. In the beginning, and now in the end, she knew that David was the only man to whom she had really and truly given that fierce, warm, wayward heart of hers. She was leaving him, not because she had stopped loving him but because she loved him too much.

For the moment, she had no plans for the future. As soon as she had finished packing she would leave a note for David, then take a taxi round to Sue's flat. Sue would make her welcome. Her friendship was unfailing. Her home would be Miranda's until she could sort things out and decide what next to do – where to go.

When finally Miranda walked out of David's studio she felt that she was leaving part of herself behind – that she would never be whole again. It seemed the end of everything.

CHAPTER THIRTEEN

It was cool and restful lying in Sue's spare bedroom. Miranda lay back on the soft pillows unable to concentrate on a new book Peter had just brought back from the library. There were flowers on either side of the dressing-table – a huge bunch of her favourite mauve and pink carnations from John and a fantastic gold basket filled with exquisite violets from David. Their perfume *en masse* like this overpowered the more exotic scent of the carnations. Their symbolism did not escape her, either. There was a bowl of fruit on the table at her side and a jug of iced orangeade.

She glanced down at the newspaper lying across the pale pink blanket.

It was the last day of September – perhaps people outside in the streets were telling each other that it was the last really warm day of summer. Not that it would make very much difference to her. She would be indoors, cut off from the rest of the world in a special hospital ward dealing with TB cases like hers. It might be a week or more before there was a bed for her. John wanted her to go home with him until the time came. But she preferred to remain here in the quiet anonymity of Sue's flat. To go home with John would be to make the final break with David and, weakened as she was by the last month of ill-health, continual coughing and the pain in her side, she did not feel she had the strength to make decisions.

Kind, generous John. He wanted to pay for a private room in the best sanatorium and was bitterly disappointed when she told him she preferred to remain independent. And David – David was as passionately attentive as any woman could wish of her lover. Filled with remorse, once he knew she had left him, he'd hurried round to Sue's flat and begged Miranda to return to him as soon as she was better. She had acute laryngitis which had attacked her the night she had arrived at Sue's place. Perhaps she might have gone, but the fates decreed that the laryngitis developed into bronchitis; then, frighteningly, came a recurrence of the TB to which she had been subject as a child.

Sue's pleasant, middle-aged doctor had told her reassuringly that this time Miranda could count on being completely cured. In the days when she'd been ill before the war, there'd been no permanent cure for TB but now, with the help of modern drugs, there was.

'We'll have you right as rain with rest and care,' he had said, patting her arm.

But after hearing the result of the X-rays and tests, she had realized that time was one of the things which couldn't be calculated accurately in cases like hers. It might be months.

'Don't think about *afterwards,* darling,' Sue had said, after Miranda had been left depleted and depressed by one of David's visits. 'You're not to worry about anything except getting well again. Frankly, Pete and I aren't the least bit surprised. You must have lost at least a couple of stone while you've been living with David; and speaking as your best friend...' she grinned disarmingly '...you've gained a few years in looks. No wonder John was so appalled the first time he saw you.'

It was Sue who had written to John when Miranda was too ill to care what was going on around her. John had come at once. Miranda had been half-conscious, with a high temperature, when she became aware that John was sitting beside her. She had been astonishingly glad to have him near – dear, dependable John. He gave her a feeling of security. Once she began to recover from the laryngitis and could talk to him, she felt grateful for his presence.

It couldn't have been easy for him, she thought, knowing she had been living with David all this time. Sue had told her that one evening the two men had met outside the flat, but John never mentioned David's name. And his conversations with Miranda were always impersonal except on the one occasion when he begged her to let him take her home.

David was so different. He exhausted her. He spoke only of their relationship – holding her hands, kissing them with passion, imposing his personality upon her. Again and again he reiterated how much he loved her, how necessary she was to his happiness, his work, his very life. But her illness seemed to have brought Miranda complete apathy. It was as though she had touched rockbottom and preferred to remain there in a vacuum rather than be pulled to the surface and be made to face life again. Sue maintained she was suffering from a nervous breakdown. Whatever it was, she could not bring herself to believe any longer in David's love, no matter how hard he protested. Nor could she believe in the happiness he promised in the future if she would but agree to go back to him. Try as she might, she could not see how anything would be different.

Sue's doctor had warned her that for some time to come she must take things easily and that she must be well looked after. David, the painter, the egoist even when he was the lover, with his busy life and constant need to travel, would have neither the time nor the inclination to 'look after' her. Whatever he might say now, he wouldn't relish a millstone round his neck; an invalid who must be considered. He would hate to have to curb his natural ebullience or keep a check on his emotions. She could see, clearly and painfully, that she could only be a handicap to him, and eventually he would regret her return. Even when she had been well, she had never really felt able to add anything of worth to his life. The hope that she would ultimately make a complete recovery could not affect the salient fact that David did not need her in the way she needed him.

She lay back against the pillows and closed her eyes. David's face, softened and tender as it sometimes was in love, haunted her. Perhaps it was best to remember him as the perfect lover and not risk seeing that face cloud over sulkily or hear the note of irritation in his voice, which had happened all too often recently. She was growing older – less able to indulge in the wild ecstasies and glories of youth.

But what kind of life could she live without him? At thirty-three she was no longer a young girl with years of youth ahead of her. Sue had remarked on her haggard looks. She didn't know if she had the strength to start building an entirely new life all over again.

The door opened. Sue came in carrying a tray of tea and two cups.

'John's just arrived. He said if you were awake, and would like it, he'd come and have tea with you. Do you want to see him?'

Miranda nodded. She didn't want to be left alone with her thoughts.

With curiosity, she watched John as he came into the room, trying to see him exactly as he really was – as though she were seeing him for the very first time. The first thought that sprang to mind was how distinguished he looked. The slight greying of his dark hair on either side of his long, aristocratic face no doubt accounted for this. A year ago there hadn't been one grey hair in that head.

Poor John! she thought. I must have made him very unhappy. *He's* aged.

He sat down in the armchair beside the bed. His dark, grave eyes studied her face rather as the doctor had done a few hours ago – a probing, searching look.

'How are you feeling, my dear? Did you manage to get a good night's sleep? I've brought you some grapes. Sue's bringing them up in a moment – the green muscats. You prefer those to the black, don't you?'

She nodded. He had taught her to appreciate the rare champagne flavour of the big green grapes with their slightly golden bloom. The tears she had been unable to shed when she left David welled into her eyes now.

'Don't pay any attention!' she said, brushing them away angrily as a child might do. 'I expect it's the drugs. They're very depressing. I'm not really crying.'

But it wasn't the drugs. It was his tender concern, his amazing acceptance of her infidelity – his constant devotion. He never forgot a preference she had voiced; and she, least of all people, deserved such solicitude.

He had not intended to bring up any mention of their relationship, but the sight of her pale, sad face – such a haunting face – completely unnerved John today. Her eyes seemed larger than ever since her illness. He felt a fierce protectiveness towards her that was part of a deep and enduring love.

He took one of her slender hands and held it tightly between his own.

'I do wish you'd let me look after you. I want you to let me fly you to Switzerland. I had a long talk with a TB specialist last night. He admits you could make a more rapid recovery up in the mountains.'

Then his voice became less restrained as his emotions took a greater hold of him.

'I know why you've said "no" so far. You don't want to feel dependent upon me in any way. But at least you could try to look on this not as my spending money on you, but as your gift to me. There would be no strings attached. It would be such a relief to me, Miranda. If, when you are fully recovered, you want to go back to David, I give my word I won't try to stop you. I know you're still in love with him but it doesn't – it won't – make any difference.'

It was a moment or two before she could trust herself to answer him. She suddenly realized that there was more than one kind of love. Her feeling for David was tempestuous, violent, demanding, calling for total surrender of the man as well as herself. But John's love was calm and unselfish. He had no thought for himself, asking nothing of her except to be able to give her back her health. He was a much finer man than David could ever be. Why, then, couldn't she love John as she loved David? What ironic whim of fate determined that she should give her heart to someone incapable of caring for it in the way that John did?

'Oh, I wish I could love you. I wish I could. I wish so much that I could!'

The cry was straight from the heart. John's reaction was instantaneous. He put out a hand and stroked back her hair as gently as if she were a sick child.

'Mandy, don't you see that if you can feel that way, it's half the battle? It was not I who wished to put an end to our old life together, although I realized even then you never loved me. The mistake I made was in not showing you just how much I loved and needed you. And *you* need to be loved perhaps more than a lot of other women do. We could be happy together. I won't ask much of you. I'll take care of you – I'll never make any demands on you. In the last resort, I've found that it doesn't even matter whether one is loved or not. It's just to be allowed to love – to give with both hands. That's how I want things to be with us.'

She was too surprised and moved to speak for a few moments. Only once had John ever spoken to her like this and that was when he first asked her to marry him. Then she had protested that she wasn't sure that she could love him in the way he had the right to expect. He had said then that it didn't matter. Maybe most of the time they had been married it hadn't mattered so much, but he must have suffered terribly. Only because he had experienced the pain, the anxiety of losing her, could he have reached a point where he could agree to separation, always hoping she would go back to him.

Haltingly, she tried to tell him so.

His lips twisted into a wry smile.

'It always mattered. I know that now. But since you've been away I've realized that in the long run it is your happiness that counts. I've found it impossible to be happy without you. I did try to find someone else. For a while it was rather pleasant to have someone in love with me ... but...' He exaggerated the words with a smile, '...but unfortunately,

I wasn't in the least in love with her and I began to find her attentions more than a little tiresome. I wanted *you* back – so much so that I sank my pride and wrote to you care of the bank. I think perhaps your visit that morning when you came to ask for a divorce – and I'd thought it was because you'd received my letter to you – was the most disappointing of my whole life. I had dared to believe that you would come back to me; and you'd only come to ask me to divorce you.'

'Don't, John,' she whispered, unable to bear the pain that lay behind his smile. It somehow seemed all wrong that this proud, fastidious man should be laying bare his heart to her. It roused in her a torrent of emotion that swept down the barrier of apathy and blank despair behind which she had managed to hide so successfully since she had fallen ill. It was not passionate love that she felt for John. It was pity for his pain and a deep sense of guilt for having brought him to his knees like this. Didn't he realize that *she wasn't worth it?* That she couldn't ever be the sort of wife he deserved?

'Thank you, dear John. I'll think about it. But you mustn't count on me. I must be absolutely honest with you. It's pointless for me to make promises I might not be able to keep. Really and truly, I don't know *what* I want. I only know that I do still love David.'

All John's instincts led him to try to

further his case, but the sight of her pale strained face, and the tears trickling through her fingers, forbade such selfishness. He clamped down on his feelings. Quietly, he said:

'Very well. I won't rush you. You will have plenty of time to think everything over carefully. I just ask you to remember this – I love you very dearly and you are free to make any conditions you wish, if you'll come back to me. I know how you feel for David. But I think you need to be loved; and I do not believe that he can give you more than I do. The security of devotion – the absolute love. Now, darling...' The endearment slipped out, '...let's talk of other things. Have you enough to read? I've ordered the new Francoise Sagan. It's light but amusing. I know you'll enjoy that. Which reminds me, I told my secretary to pack up a pile of magazines and paperbacks. Have they arrived?'

She could not answer. She was crying.

Soon after Sue brought in the grapes, John left. He did not kiss Miranda good-bye, but he held her hand for a moment and promised to come back tomorrow.

The room seemed emptier and lonelier to Miranda after he had gone, and she was glad when Sue returned to draw the curtains and switch on the lights.

'Is David coming this evening?' she asked, as she plumped up the pillows and moved the tea-tray.

Miranda nodded.

'You know, the more I see of your John, the more I like him,' Sue went on.

'I like him, too,' Miranda said with a deep sigh.

Sue grimaced.

'H'm. But as a friend – not a husband. Oh, I admit that David has all the charm, that certain something which can catch and hold a woman's heart. But although it's none of my business, let me at least remind you, Mandy darling, if you're trying to make up your mind what to do, that living with David made you very, very unhappy. Don't go back to him, please. Don't let him persuade you that you're the only thing in the world that matters to him. He finds it easy to say such things, and I think he means them at the time. But they just aren't true, Mandy.'

'I dare say, but somehow it doesn't seem to make much difference. You see, my commonsense tells me to go back to John and feel sure of him and life. But I don't think that would be fair since I could not love John as I do love David. It's as simple as that.'

'Why let it matter so much? John would be sufficiently rewarded by the pleasure of taking care of you. That's the sort of person he is. You know, Mandy, you're still young enough to have children. You may have managed to convince yourself in the past that you didn't want to be tied down by motherhood, but I remember that day in hospital when Melanie was born. You told me you'd achieved your dearest ambition. After she died, you deliberately trod on the maternal side of your nature. You managed to convince yourself that children would never again be important to you. If you went back to John and had a baby, I believe you'd be happy. During these last few days I've learned enough about John to believe that he is one hundred percent a family man. It would be a family unit – something new and fine and worthwhile. Think about it Mandy.'

But after Sue left her alone once more, Miranda realized that Sue's answer to her problem was no more complete than John's. It was true that she *would* like a child, *but it was David's child, not John's, that she wanted...*

She tried to sleep before David came. His visits always exhausted her and left her emotionally drained. He could not sit down quietly by her bedside but walked up and down the room, tormenting her and himself by analysing their relationship until she could no longer think clearly.

Tonight he was the same, his personality filling the room, his strong square frame seeming to tower over her bed as he looked down at her. His narrow, critical eyes were demanding, fiery, possessive.

'Pete told me that John's been here again. You can't be thinking about going back to him. It would be madness, Mandy. You weren't happy with him before. You belong to me, and you know it.'

He picked up a book, flicked through the pages, frowning, and flung it down again, restless, pacing. The fact that Miranda had suddenly become difficult to get had renewed his earlier passion to possess her. Jealousy was a new emotion for him since women were not in the habit of leaving him for other men. Only Miranda had dared to do this – not once, it would seem, but twice! It bit at his pride – his ego.

She looked so entrancing, ethereally lovely and fragile since her illness; the tell-tale flush of her condition coloured her cheeks; her eyes were unnaturally large and bright. He wanted to get her back to the studio and paint her as *La Dame aux Camellias* – the courtesan who had died of love and consumption.

'You swore to me that first night you spent in the studio that you would never leave me again. Why won't you tell me what I did to upset or disappoint you? Why weren't you happy? You knew I didn't love Deborah. Were you just angry because I had to spend so much time with Douna and Jonathan? I should have thought you were above such petty jealousies, Mandy. You must have known that all the time I wanted to be back with you, my sweet, sweet Mandy.'

She struggled to reason with him. If only she felt stronger!

'I suppose I *was* jealous of your wife and child, David. I found that I'm incapable of sharing the man I love – with *anyone,* anything. None of this is your fault – you mustn't ever think so. This time, I'm the one who has failed. I thought that even a little of you would be better than nothing, but I was wrong. I was far too possessive.'

David walked across to the window. He stared down into the street below. He was momentarily nonplussed by Miranda's admission that she was to blame. He'd been feeling uncomfortably guilty ever since he'd returned to the studio to find her gone and then heard from Sue that she was so desperately ill. He'd decided to wait until she was sufficiently recovered to talk everything over and defend himself, although he'd never been quite sure why he must do so. After all, Miranda had known he was married, known he'd be forced to leave her on occasions. It wasn't as if he'd cheated her or neglected her unduly.

Why, he asked himself angrily, must women be so confoundedly possessive? He was in the devil of a position with Douna clinging and Miranda demanding. Obviously, he was going to be forced to choose between them.

He swung round and looked at Miranda with accusation in his eyes.

'I suppose you want me to make Douna divorce me. Is that what you're getting at; remarriage for us?'

This idea, oddly enough, had never once occurred to Miranda. For a moment, her heart leapt in a great surge of hope. If they could be married ... but in the same instant, she knew that such a marriage would solve nothing. The legal tie hadn't kept David faithful to Douna. The paper security of a marriage certificate would guarantee her nothing. Nor was there any hope that she would find peace of mind if she tried to build her future out of the pieces of another woman's marriage. No – let Douna keep what was so important to her. She, Miranda, would never take *that* away.

She looked up at David's attractive, sulky face. He looked so much like a small boy who had been told that he cannot have both cake and jam for tea. Suddenly, she realized just how ruthless David was. For all his earlier insistences that he could not hurt Douna, now that he thought he might lose her, Miranda, he was prepared to go back on that; prepared to wave aside poor Douna as if she were of no consequence because she stood between him and what he wanted.

He was completely self-centred. How then was it possible to go on loving such a man? Even now, she knew that if he approached the bedside, her arms would reach out involuntarily to him. Was this great love she felt, any more than a strong physical attraction? The thought appalled Miranda. It was so degrading to go on wanting a man physically when you could no longer respect him. It was more than degrading to have to admit that the whole pattern of her life had been woven round a myth – an illusion. Yet didn't other women love men who were 'no good'? The wives of murderers, of alcoholics, even of rapists, remained pathetically faithful to them; they stood by men who were repeatedly unfaithful, who abused them. How was it possible to distinguish between love and a lasting infatuation, or were they one and the same?

She was suddenly frightened; frightened of David's angry voice, his overwhelming presence. He was a cruel laughing devil about to sweep her back into temptation – into hell. She was afraid he would come forward, touch her and like a wizard cast a fresh spell upon her until she was powerless to resist him, until she could no longer see him as the man he really was. She felt quite helpless and unable to defend herself against the tremendous force of his personality. She wanted to tell him to leave her alone – in peace. The words stuck in her throat. Then suddenly a new terror struck her. She tried to speak and no sound came. Her throat seemed to have closed up. She was dumb. Every vestige of colour left her face. She did not know it but this time the trouble was self-induced. It had, however, the desired effect, because David stopped ranting.

He looked down at her in deep concern, then scared of what he saw, ran to the door and called to Sue:

'For God's sake phone your doctor quickly. Mandy's been taken ill again. I think she's had a relapse.'

Cutting from THE SUNDAY NEWS, September 1962

David Leyland, the well-known portrait painter, left London Airport yesterday for the Bahamas. He told our reporter that he is to paint Miss Shelley Ristali, the actress, at her home in Nassau. Mr Leyland was accompanied by a beautiful mysterious fair-haired model, who refused to identify herself but who has been seen with him on many occasions recently. Mr Leyland says we shall see portraits of his companion and Miss Ristali at his next Exhibition.

Cutting from THE WEEKLY GLOBE, October 1962

Pictured going aboard the newly-built 'FRANCE', now the longest ship in the world –

Mr John Villiers, well-known finance expert and his lovely wife. They were sailing for New York where Mr Villiers will be attending to business for a few days after which he and Mrs Villiers plan to spend the winter in the Caribbean.

Miranda sat in her deck-chair, a rug tucked around her legs, her eyes not on the wide expanse of green ocean but on the man leaning over the rail. What was John thinking, she wondered? She had tried so many times during her convalescence to understand her feelings. More than anything in the world, she wanted John to know that she had allowed him back into her life not because she needed him but because she loved him; because she had grown up at last and meant to spend the rest of her life making up to him those six wasted years.

At the nursing home and later at home, whilst she regained her strength, John had taken complete charge and one of his orders had been that they would discuss their future only once they were aboard the 'FRANCE' and not until then. 'You need the holiday – and there's no hurry!' he had said each time she had tried to broach the subject. She had been too weak to argue that if this was to be a permanent reconciliation, then she owed it to him to explain, to ask his forgiveness.

Now that she was almost completely restored to health, she was impatient to reassure him that her change of heart had nothing to do with David's behaviour. Would John understand? Was it too much to expect when she was only just beginning to understand herself how wrong she had been to believe that the 'high's and low's' of a love affair were what she wanted, needed? She had mistaken those intense moments of excitement and passion for ... for the kind of love on which marriages are founded. Once she had complained to John that they were more like friends who sometimes went to bed together. Now at last she understood how important that friendship was; how in the end it had always been John who was there to love and cherish her no matter how small a part of her heart she had given to him. Now at last she had discovered how much there was to love about the man she had married, and she would be the one to change the physical side of their relationship. She had only to see the look in John's eyes these past few days to know that he was capable of the kind of passion that would match her own.

Somehow, she must let him know that it was her fault if in the past he had kept that side of his nature in restraint, for she had never given that side of herself to him as once she had to David – and perhaps to Ludwig.

She felt a moment of deep anxiety as John turned and came towards her. Would she be able to find the words – the right words?

As he stood there looking down at her, she realised suddenly that now – as it had always been – John had solved the matter for her. There was no need for her to speak, to explain.

'Of all the women in the world, to me you are the most beautiful and by far the most desirable,' he said in a low urgent voice. 'If I were married to another woman, I swear to God I would be unfaithful to her – with you my darling.'

As he led her hurriedly towards the privacy of their state-room, she knew that all those impossible dreams, those deepest needs of her heart were about to be fulfilled.

The publishers hope that this book has given you enjoyable reading. Large Print Books are especially designed to be as easy to see and hold as possible. If you wish a complete list of our books please ask at your local library or write directly to:

Dales Large Print Books
Magna House, Long Preston,
Skipton, North Yorkshire.
BD23 4ND

This Large Print Book, for people
who cannot read normal print,
is published under the auspices of

THE ULVERSCROFT FOUNDATION

... we hope you have enjoyed this book.
Please think for a moment about those
who have worse eyesight than you ...
and are unable to even read or enjoy
Large Print without great difficulty.

You can help them by sending a
donation, large or small, to:

**The Ulverscroft Foundation,
1, The Green, Bradgate Road,
Anstey, Leicestershire, LE7 7FU,
England.**
or request a copy of our brochure for
more details.

The Foundation will use all donations
to assist those people who are visually
impaired and need special attention
with medical research, diagnosis
and treatment.

Thank you very much for your help.